KATIE BULLER

Light In The Dark Room

"Sydney, when you find your person, never let them go."

Eden Monroe

1

Sydney

This city is always gloomy. Grey skies, grey buildings, just bleak. There is nothing attractive or remotely appealing about New York. Everyone else seems to think it is wonderful. "The city of opportunities," they say. Not for me.

My life began in rural England and it ended in New York City.

I have been stuck in this hellish townhouse for days. The winter flu season is in full force. Everywhere you go people are sneezing or spluttering and it is frankly just another reason to despise New York.

I sigh. My father slams the door on his way to work and Brianna is blasting music in her room. "There is not a single moment of peace in this awful place," I groan, turning over to face the wall.

In that moment, I can't tell what I'm more cross about – the fact that I am still stuck in this modern, brown, terraced prison, or the fact that my father has forgotten about me for the third day in a row.

Let me rephrase. The third day in a row, in this streak.

The last one went on for a whole fifteen days before he acknowledged me or Brianna. But who's counting?

In a strange way, I've always admired his resilience, his ability to forget everything that happened without a care in the world. I wish I could forget like he does. But my love for her and the pain of knowing that she is gone forever, stops me in my tracks whenever I try to move on.

I wish I could stop my emotions colliding, chipping away at the wall I have worked so hard to build up. I wish that I could stop caring, stop crying. But most of all, I just wish that she would come back to me. Back to us.

I'm sure that under dad's bravado he's a broken man. If only he would let someone in long enough to discover how he has really been feeling these past years.

When I was sick, she used to hold me until I fell asleep. I miss that. We would listen to the birds outside of my window and she would hum softly as she stroked my soft hair into place. Everything was perfect back then. Or at least, I thought it was.

In reality though, she was fading, even at that point.

"God, I will not cry. Not today." I breathe in as deeply as I can, hoping that my lungs begin to function once again.

"Come on, Sydney, snap out of it." I am angry now. Angry at myself, angry at my dad, angry at the world. But most of all, I am angry that she left me.

"I can come back later if now is a bad time." My little sister is loitering by the door, chewing her lip. I hadn't even heard her turn the music off upstairs, let alone her quiet footsteps padding along the wooden panelled floor to my room.

"No, Bri, it's fine." I tug at the hem of my shirt, wondering how much she had witnessed of my momentary blip in sanity.

Although, even if she had seen everything, she wouldn't mention it. No one in this house ever mentions feelings. It's an unspoken family rule that no one dares to break.

"What do you want?"

She bit her lip again, teeth piercing the soft skin, as she fights the question on her lips. "Where's dad?"

I roll my eyes. "Out."

Her eyes sink to the floor in disappointment, although I don't know why this revelation would shock her. He's always out. Always working.

"Oh, I see, well -" she starts again, before stopping and gazing wistfully at the floor. "Okay, well, I'm going to meet Avery for a bit."

She falters by the door, as if searching desperately for my approval. I shrug at her. It's not that I don't care, I just don't feel well and a bit of quiet time without her clattering her way through a pop soundtrack seems ideal.

She leaves as quietly as she came and I flop back onto my bed, resting my palm against my temple.

"This is stupid. There has got to be something I can do in this place." I scan the untouched trinkets and books that have sat dormant above my head for years. An old, battered book catches my eye, sitting alone at one end of the forgotten shelf.

When we first arrived in the city, my father got rid of every little resemblance of her he could find. No box remained untouched during his rampage, no physical memory of her left intact.

He always said he had thrown them away, but I have my doubts. I've seen letters from the storage locker. I know he has hidden them away, out of sight.

The thought of her belongings hauled up in a damp, dark

locker gives me the shivers, but it's nowhere near as bad as the thought of her things being bitten and torn apart in a refuse centre. So, I leave it alone, for the sake of holding onto whatever remnants of peace this family clings onto.

Finding every ounce of strength, the illness has left in my body, I make my way across the creaking floorboards to the neatly arranged shelves. I take a moment to appreciate just how much stuff I had forgotten about long ago.

The thought hasn't even finished processing however, when I lock eyes with the target. Leaning up, I pull the book off the shelf. A flurry of dust follows it as I choke, fighting for air, in amongst the plume of long forgotten particles.

Spluttering back to my bed, I inspect the book thoroughly as it rests in my hands, removing the remaining dust from its casing. The cover looks worn, like the book had been loved for decades. The writing is fading elegantly, but there is absolutely no mistaking.

This is it.

I stare at the book and blink twice, expecting it to vanish like the cloud of dust it came with. But it doesn't. It is real and I can't believe it.

I allow myself a small, triumphant grin, as I comprehend that this book somehow escaped the vicious cleaning spree that my father conducted years ago.

My once steady breathing stops as I open the book and flick through its tired pages. The words scrawled across each page and the colours in the pictures fill me with life as I exhale once more.

Calmness washes over me as I am transported back to a time when life was simpler.

Little Red Riding Hood. My childhood obsession. The book I

– no – we, would read every single day without fail.

I soak in the musky scent - the familiarity of home still lingering within its very foundations.

Holding this book makes me wonder something I haven't dared to ask myself for years, in fear of disappointment. What other gems hide in the depths of dad's stupid secret locker?

The thought makes my skin crawl and I shudder, trying to lose myself in the story again. I read from the beginning. The nostalgia hits me in waves. I trace each word gently with my finger, study each beautiful illustration with precision and care.

It feels like it's the first time I have ever laid eyes on this beautiful book. Yet, it isn't. I continue my journey through the pages, becoming more elated with every twist and turn.

With each new word that I digest, reminders hit me, triggering memories that usually I would force down and bury. But maybe that was the old me?

This book, being so close to her in these pages, bridges the gap that my heart has felt for over a decade. I can't believe this has been there, right on that shelf, all this time and I haven't bothered to look.

Okay, the shelf isn't at eye level, but if I had just taken the chance to look around and stop, I would have seen it.

My head drops involuntarily to my chest as the pages become fewer and fewer. As I turn the last page, an immense wave of sadness floods over me.

I wish I could go back, just twenty minutes. I wish I could experience all those first-time emotions on repeat.

My bliss subsides in an instant as I move away from the comfort of my bed to place the book back on the shelf. This time, however, I vow not to abandon it for another decade, before reaching up and slotting the book into its former position.

As I return to the comfort of my bed, my gaze shifts towards something lying at my feet. I breathe sharply as an inscription comes into view.

"Sydney. You bring the colour into my world."

I recognise the handwriting instantly. How could I forget it? My hands quiver as I lower my body slowly to pick up the paper.

Tracing my fingers over the inscription, I am distracted by the distinct markings that surround it. As I turn the page in my hands, I gasp.

A photograph. But not just any photograph. One in colour.

My mother never took her pictures in colour. She believed that photography should be kept in its original form and that altering it in any way was wrong.

"It's all about the personal connection to the art you have created, Sydney," she would say, on an almost daily basis.

I remember her telling me that as clear as day, when I questioned why exactly we had been sitting in the dark room for hours, developing her prints. She would swear by it. As far as I knew, she never took a single colour photo in her life. Black and white was all I knew. All she knew.

Until today.

2

Freddie

"Freddie!"

I groan. Hearing my mother's tired and feeble voice first thing in the morning is enough to make anyone wake up in a foul mood.

I used to love the way she called my name, but her tone has changed. Come to think of it, everything has changed – and I can't cope with yet another reminder of what he is doing to her.

I roll over in bed, my fuzzy hair sticking up on end as I rub my eyes. I figure that if it's important, she will come up here.

She doesn't though. She never does. I think seeing me lying here in this dingy room makes her feel guilty and she can't bear that. Not on top of everything else she has to deal with.

I hear the door close softly behind her. It's impossible to miss in this tiny flat, unless you have passed out from a night of heavy drinking, that is.

My father. Grant. The single biggest waste of space I have ever laid my eyes on.

I grimace at the recollection of how my mother used to be, the fond memories short-lived and the realisation hits. She will never be the same, but then again, neither will I.

Despite my misgivings about the alarm clock by my bed still radiating the number five, I drag my weary body out of bed. I hate leaving this early, but for me, early rising is essential.

If I am going to raise enough money to move out of this hellhole anytime soon, I need to take every job opportunity thrown my way. That means early mornings and even later nights.

"Is any of this worth it?" I mumble into the night. My questioning doesn't last long, however. The sight of Grant slumped across the mattress through the crack in the door is the only answer I need.

Freedom. That's all I want from my life. I think that's all anyone wants. Freedom and happiness. I currently possess neither. And that needs to change.

Thankfully, it doesn't take me long to get ready and I'm out the door in no time, slamming it loudly behind me, hoping to give Grant his daily wake-up call. Whether it works, I have no idea. He must get up sometime though, because by the time I get home he's gone. He's always gone.

I have lived in New York all my life and yet it still never fails to surprise me with how busy it is. It's five forty-five in the morning. The streets are bustling, taxis hooting and commuters chattering as they jostle for position on the sidewalk.

God, I hate this city.

I trudge along, avoiding eye contact with every pedestrian I pass for fear that they will see the mess that lurks behind the suit and tie.

As my office building comes into sight, I silently thank New York geography that my work is only two blocks away. Public transport is far too expensive and I really don't fancy walking miles for a mediocre job that just pays the bills.

"Ah, Mr Robinson!" Mason grins at me as I swing through the revolving doors and into the blinding bright lobby. How he has this much energy this early in the morning really is beyond my comprehension.

"Mason." I nod, hoping that he'll give me my schedule and leave. In true New Yorker fashion though, he doesn't. He's Mason and he's hellbent on becoming my friend.

Let me make this clear, I don't do friends. Or any close relationships for that matter. All they do is hurt you.

He follows me into my small office, still grinning, his mouth stretching his face in new ways I never believed possible. I have never met anyone who smiles like Mason does.

"Luke wants you in his office at ten." Mason wiggles his eyebrows at me and continues his attempt at making me smile. "You've got a new project, how exciting!" Mason tries again.

He receives an eye roll in return, my standard morning response. "How exciting," I mumble under my breath, before turning on my desktop and pretending to respond to an email in the hope he'd eventually leave me alone. He does, ambling cheerfully out of my office and closing the door gently behind him.

Sighing in relief, I allow myself a small smile. Lucas is giving me a new project and I've only just finished the last one. He must have really liked my work on the Brooklyn annual art competition.

Truth be told, I am thrilled at the recognition. I wasn't expecting another project so soon. Projects like these pay the bills, allow me to save. Projects like these are my lifeline.

The morning passes quickly and I am grateful for that. My job without projects is dull and until Lucas gives me my latest assignment, I am stuck on admin.

I thrive under the pressure of deadlines. I am good at building a façade where no one knows me. It is something I have been practising for over ten years now. I love appearing confident, putting on a mask and being cool for once. I love how it makes me feel. It makes me feel alive.

Ten to ten and I am already waiting for Lucas outside his office. I know full well that he isn't there. He'll be sipping his morning coffee in a board meeting with the executives. But I am just too excited to hear about my next project.

I hope it is something modern. I adore modern art. It's so expressive, so vibrant and has the habit of making even the saddest person happy, even momentarily.

I spot Mason in the distance, surrounded by a group of our colleagues. They are all laughing, having a good time. I don't even know most of their names. It rarely bothers me, but today it makes me feel like I'm missing out.

I know there is more to life than this small bubble I inhabit, but expanding it would mean disrupting my comfort zone. Lots of people in my bubble would be catastrophic. It just takes one person to take out a pin and pop, it all falls apart. My entire life falls apart. I can't go through that again.

I am snapped out of my daydream by Lucas's heavy footsteps trudging down the corridor towards me. Mason gives me a thumbs up and goofy grin from behind him. I fight a small smile before turning to Lucas and following him into his office.

"Right, Robinson. Let's do this." Authority radiates from every word he speaks.

His office is much nicer than mine and is something I aspire to. Plush chairs litter the soft carpet by the oak desk. Artwork adorns the walls and a state-of-the-art computer takes pride of place on the table.

"Robinson," he begins. "As I am sure you are aware by now, your latest coverage really impressed me." I look down at my hands. I know better than to interrupt Lucas, even to say thank you, when he is in full swing.

"I have a new project that needs coverage for the November edition and you are the perfect man for the job." Again, I felt a surge of pride sweep over me. I have given my everything to this job, so to finally get some recognition is a wonderful achievement.

"I need you to cover a brand-new event taking place in Brooklyn in two weeks' time. It's a vintage art exhibition. I know how much you loved the last exhibition we sent you to."

My heart sinks. A vintage art exhibition? Vintage? "But Lucas, I -" I try to get the words out, but nothing comes. I need this too much.

"Great! I knew you would be excited! Do some research, propose some stories and have it on my desk by next week."

I look at my feet as I try to form a sentence, but words fail me. I gawp at him like an idiot. "Don't let me down, Robinson." Luke's eyes burn into me as he waves me out of his office, before turning back to his computer and continuing to type.

I walk back to my office in a daze. I can't even remember how I got there, but when my body slumps into my creaking chair, reality hits. I know nothing about vintage art. I hate vintage art. I am a modernist lover, through and through. I thought Lucas knew that.

I rest my hands against the cold, bumpy surface of my desk, looking around my office, contemplating how much of a sin it would be to refuse the job. Probably career ending is the conclusion I arrive at.

I can't lose this job. I have worked too damn hard to get to this point. That's the only reason I sit down at my computer and research my assignment.

Information is scarce, but I eventually cobble together enough to begin a proposal. The event itself is being held at an old, converted warehouse in Brooklyn.

I groan loudly as I scan over the date. The 20th October only gives me seven days to write my piece and send it to the editor for approval in the November issue.

I compile everything I find into a fact file, along with some photographic references to the art that will display. There are antique sculptures, vintage cameras, ancient paintings and an old black and white or sepia photography section.

To me it lacks colour and excitement. I like my art to convey genuine feeling and fill people with wonder. The only thing this artwork, in all its dull tones, will make people feel, is bored.

By the time my lunch break rolls around, I am fed up. I grab my things and take off to the one place I really love in this city. The one place that makes me feel my true self.

3

Sydney

I pace my room, wearing down the old wooden floorboards with every step, desperately trying to control the anger towards my father rising inside my body.

I know it is irrational, but after finding that photo, that inscription, my mind has been a mess and I am out of control. I need answers and I need clarity. He has those answers and he has been keeping them from me for too long. Today he has nowhere left to hide.

He will lie to me, tell me that her things have long since been destroyed. He might even get angry. No, wait, he won't. He won't get angry because that would mean showing emotion and my father doesn't do that.

My family has buried their heads in the sand ever since mum died and that must change. At least, it must change for me. Brianna was too little to remember her properly at just five years old.

My mum, our mum, was the best we could have wished for. A shining light in a very dark world.

I never got closure. Dad shipped the entire family off to New York in pursuit of a new life before we could even properly say goodbye. So, whatever is in that storage locker –

The front door creaks open. I know it isn't Bri. She's out with Avery until tomorrow. So, I gather every ounce of courage I can muster and stride down the stairs. I want to appear confident, determined, strong. I feel the opposite.

Truth be told, I have never been good at conflict, so I pray that this act is good enough to get through to him. I pray that I don't look like the fraud I feel.

"Dad!" I yell in the most authoritative voice I can muster. I know that by calling for him, I am taking him by surprise. I never call for him. In fact, we rarely have conversations that last longer than a few words.

He tiptoes up the stairs towards my room. I can tell he is apprehensive as he rests his hand against the door frame and shuffles his feet into the wood.

"Hello... Um... Sydney... How are you?" He blinks rapidly and waits for my response. Being a father does not come naturally to my dad.

I take a gulp of oxygen and glare at him defiantly. "Where are mum's things?"

In an instant his features change. His eyes are dark and wide with panic. His skin pales as he chews into his lip. At least I now know where Brianna got that awful habit from.

"I don't know what you mean," he eventually utters. But I can tell that he knows the game is up. Frustration courses through my veins. How dare he lie to my face? He loved mum just as much as I do.

Maybe that's the problem. Loved. Maybe he doesn't love her anymore. Maybe he resents her for leaving. Or maybe he just doesn't want to remember.

I shake the thoughts away with a shudder. Of course he loves her.

"The key fob in your bag, the letters from the storage locker and the code that you have written in your diary." I brandish the letter in his face, as his skin turns from pale to translucent.

He looks tired, almost as though this is a battle he doesn't have the energy to fight anymore. I hadn't noticed it before. He hadn't been in the same room long enough for me to notice. He looks like a ghost.

I feel a pang of sympathy. This feeling however, is short-lived, as he turns on his heel and walks away, leaving me standing alone, dumbstruck.

I stalk after him down the stairs, reaching the landing as the door to his office slams shut.

His office is where he always hides. He spends his life there. I always used to wonder what was so interesting in that stupid room that made him want to spend more time there than with his family. But after a while I just stopped caring.

"No," I yell, barging through the door and startling him. "You do not get to walk away from me, not this time."

The brick wall turns to face me. "There is no storage locker, Sydney. Now leave. I'm working."

Fed up with playing his silly games, I march to his bag, flung carelessly against a chair in the corner of the room and grab it before he has the chance to react.

I ransack its contents until I find the fob and diary I was looking for. "Thank you," I hiss sarcastically and slam my way back out of the door.

I can hear him contemplating whether to follow me, pacing and muttering in his damned office. I don't give him the chance to follow though. I am out the front door like a rocket, grabbing a coat as I fly through.

I don't stop running until I've reached the promenade. My father has never taken the time to explore Brooklyn. He probably doesn't even know that there is a promenade, let alone how to get to it.

Feeling safe and out of reach, I lower myself onto a bench and thumb through the diary.

Work appointments, software passwords, meetings. I am getting frustrated now. As I turn the last page of his diary, I see it.

The code and a Manhattan address. My heart sinks. He couldn't even store her things in Brooklyn. All this time I have been separated from my mum by a bridge and I had no idea.

I had only ever crossed the bridge for two purposes: for college and now for work. Both of which are adequate reasons to despise that bridge.

I heave myself up from the bench and make my way to the Brooklyn Bridge – loved by tourists, hated by me. Yet it has now become the pathway to my mum.

I use the chance to examine it and discover, to my surprise, that it really is beautiful. In this moment all I feel is freedom. Excitement. It replaces the usual feelings of dread and hatred as I drive by in a pre-booked car.

I set my sights on the Manhattan skyline and walk. As I near the end, the bridge becomes busier, more crowded. I don't think Brooklyn ever gets this busy and for that I am grateful.

Despite the busyness, there is an air of anonymity on this side of the bridge. No one knows who I am and I love it. On our street in Brooklyn Heights, everyone knows everyone.

I look around me as I reach the other side and step onto

Manhattan soil. A woman catches my eye. She is dressed in plain, grey clothes and has a look of sadness etched into her delicate skin.

She is looking at the bridge, almost as if deliberating whether to cross. She doesn't. She walks away, each step slow and painful. I watch as she fades from view, wondering what her story is.

It is so interesting – we pass so many people during our lifetimes and yet we will know so few of their stories. I continue to ponder this as I wander through the streets. I look at passers-by, wonder who they are, what they are going through. Everyone seems in such a rush and yet, if people just stopped and took a moment to just exist, the world would be so much happier.

I stare intently at the maps on my phone, trying desperately to navigate the streets. It is so easy to get lost in this borough. I wonder if my father would notice if I didn't come back.

My phone vibrates again, letting me know that my desti-nation is on the left. The building is grim. He wouldn't leave mum's things here, surely?

I push through the heavy doors. The interior is just as unfriendly as the outside. In the foyer there is a single desk with two burly men standing behind it.

"Locker 24A, please."

4

Freddie

City Hall Park, New York is the only place I feel myself. An unusual choice in a place so large, I know. But there is something calming about sitting by the fountain and getting lost in the sound of the falling water.

It is my favourite place in the city and has been since I can remember. Every day, after a busy morning at the office, I come here and think.

I must look so weird to my fellow New Yorkers, just sitting, staring into the cascades. This park is hardly a place one would typically sit and think.

I don't care though. I don't care because it is the one part of the day that is my own. The one time I get to put myself first and not think about work, or my parents, or even finding a flat. I simply take time to exist.

As I sit in the park, watching the water, I notice the world going by. Parents are walking with their children. They look so cheerful. An elderly couple are sitting opposite me, resting on a bench. I envy them. They look as though they have all the time in the world.

The time flies, as usual. I always dread going back to work after my lunch break. A time filled with so much calm always comes abruptly to a halt as soon as I leave the park. As soon as I cross the threshold, my outer persona is back and for another twenty-four hours, I am no longer myself.

I head back through the office doors, keeping my head down, to avoid unnecessary conversation. I spy Mason in the corner with the same group of colleagues as earlier. I dash past. I'm not surprised. They eat lunch together every day without fail.

Mason has tried to get me to join them on more occasions than I care to count. But the answer is always a firm and resounding no.

"Did you have a good lunch?" he calls after me cheerfully as I head to my office. "Yep," is the only response he gets.

I slump back down into my chair and stare at the screen. The sight of the art exhibition fact-file I had spent the whole morning compiling popping up makes my blood boil. I normally find my job tolerable, but this project makes me feel the opposite. It makes me want to walk out and say to hell with it.

As much as I despise vintage art however, I despise living with my parents more.

"What?" I snap, a knocking at the door disturbing my workflow. "There is no way I am going to finish this now." I trudge towards the door.

Mason's smile gleams at me, his expression hopeful. Normally it would be a challenge to prevent his cheerful demeanour from chipping away at my own rigid exterior, but today it's easy.

"Freddo!" I glare at him. I have told him at least a thousand times not to call me that. But he never listens.

I am not in the mood to deal with him today and at this point I am seriously considering slamming the door in his face. I resist the temptation. As much as I am annoyed by his presence, I really do like Mason. Even if I don't admit it.

"Fred, you've kept yourself hidden away in this office all afternoon." He helps himself to my chair, spinning around on it twice before steadying himself and giving me a big goofy grin.

"I know. This is an office. It's called working," I reply sarcastically. Mason studies me for a second, that stupid grin of his never once leaving his face.

"You're coming out tonight and I'm not taking no for an answer. Faye and I are going to see a movie." I stare at him blankly, lost for words at how ridiculous and yet hopeful he can be.

"Mason, whatever makes you think I want to watch a movie with you and your girlfriend?" I have never once gone out with him and yet now he decides he has the right to insist.

Happy couples make me sick and Mason and Faye are the happiest couple I know. I would rather go home and listen to my parents argue for three hours than watch a film with a happy couple.

Mason is staring at me now and I feel my façade beginning to crumble. What if he can see through me? What if he knows what I'm hiding?

It is unnerving to have someone try to break my guard. Mason hasn't said a word. He is still gazing intently, eyes blazing, trying to uncover the real man behind the mask.

"Look, Mason, you go and have a good time. I have work to do tonight, but maybe some other time? Yeah?" I immediately feel awkward in the silence, which is unusual for me, as I usually prefer it.

"You mean that?" His face lights up, full of hope and excitement. He has been trying to include me since I started at this job. I can tell he counts this as a victory.

"Yeah, of course," I say with as much enthusiasm as I can muster. I hate lying to Mason. I hate lying in general, but it's the only way I can think to get out of this situation.

A strange, unknown feeling hits me, as I fight the flicker of emotion trying to cross my face. The feeling is short-lived. But it is there. And I felt it.

"Well, goodnight then Fred." He waves goodbye and gets up from the chair, never breaking that warm and friendly smile.

As soon as he leaves, I exhale, allowing myself a moment's peace. While I'm not ready to let anyone into my life, it is nice to know that somebody cares.

I look down at the battered watch clinging tightly to my wrist. I don't believe I have ever left work this early before. It is a surreal feeling, walking the streets of New York when it isn't dark. I'm so used to power walking to get home as soon as is physically possible, but today, under the light of dusk, I can take my time.

I look around me as I walk, instead of looking straight down at my shoes. I take the time to notice people walking by. I even return the smile of a few strangers. It feels nice to feel like a part of a bigger picture, rather than isolated, even if it is just for a second.

As I reach the flat, my sense of calm and happiness falters. He won't be there. I know he won't. But it doesn't stop me from tiptoeing up the stairs and opening the door to the flat a lot more quietly than I usually would.

The flat is empty, just as I expected. Dad will be putting in early orders at a bar he can't afford. And mom will be working yet another night shift to fund his habits and our rent.

I throw my bag down onto the mattress and stare helplessly at the ceiling.

What is wrong with me? I never normally let any of this get to me. Why should today be any different? I blink furiously and stare at a single spot above me. I do not cry.

I didn't cry when all of this started. I didn't cry when he yelled for the first time. I will not cry now.

"He wasn't always like this. He didn't always hate me," I whisper into the air.

"Eva!" my father bellows, slamming into our furniture as he enters the flat. The door crashes shut behind him and I leap to my feet.

"Get out here!" He's never home this early. Something must have happened. I hold my breath, praying that he'll leave before the neighbours file another noise complaint.

The silence deafens as he stumbles around in the dark, presumably looking for my mom. The only sound, his shabby boots, scuffing the old wood floor.

"She isn't here." I flick the switch, flooding the flat in a golden light, exposing the pathetic man in front of me for the first time.

I keep the breath I have been holding, not wanting to move or make a sound. It's not that he scares me, not like he used to. I'm not a child now. He does, however, make me feel uncomfortable, so I do my best to avoid any confrontation.

I take a moment to study my father, the man I used to idolise. He looks different. His hair is tangled and matted against his forehead, eyes dark and sunken. He looks exhausted.

He stinks of beer. I wrinkle my nose up at the disgusting smell that fills the flat. I am never, ever, going to drink.

"Why not?" he growls, throwing his hands up into the air in frustration. "Where is she then?"

I clench my fists. How dare he speak about my mother like that? She works tirelessly day and night to keep a roof over this family's head and this is how he treats her.

"She is out working, keeping you in beer money." My eyes narrow and I spit my words out, not wanting to speak to him for any longer than I must.

He is looking me up and down now with a permanent scowl fixed across his worn face. I feel dirty under his gaze. I wish he wouldn't look at me. I wish I had the power to step up and kick him out for good, tell him to never come back.

Although, even if I did, he wouldn't listen. He never does. The only way to get rid of him for good is for mom to divorce him and that will never happen.

He doesn't respond, simply grabbing a fistful of notes from the counter and staggering back out the door. My mother's wages, gone. Just like that.

5

Sydney

"Locker 24A is the third on the right." One of the burly security guards points me toward the dingy corridor.

I nod a small thank you in reply and head in the direction he has just pointed. The corridor is cold and damp, with a series of bleak, metal doors.

As I reach the door, shivers run through my body. The fob slots against the keypad and unlocks it with ease, revealing a series of numbers. Numbers that will unlock this door and bring me closer to my mum.

3074.

The door creaks against my touch. I continue to push against the cold metal before setting my sights on boxes and boxes of things. My mum's whole life in this cold, dark room.

An overwhelming sadness builds inside me. How could he just abandon her here? Did he even bring her things here himself? Surely, he wouldn't have been comfortable leaving her life here in nothing more than a dark stone box.

I take a minute to steady myself before sitting on the floor next to the mountain of boxes. Maybe this was a mistake. Maybe I'm just not ready to see this. My hands are shaking as I brush them gently against the boxes.

Seeing all of this has made me realise one thing though. There is no way I have the capacity to rescue all these things from this locker. At least not now.

I place my hand on the first box, gently opening the flaps. He hasn't even sealed them properly. I brush the dust from the items hidden below, revealing a pile of clothes.

I grab a jumper from the top of the pile and hug it tightly against my chest. I feel tears pricking at my eyes as the realisation hits me. This is the closest I can get to my mum now. I put the jumper back carefully and sort through the boxes again.

There are lots of boxes of clothes and a few with knick-knacks from her shop in them, but nothing deeply personal. I'm looking for things that truly represent her, not just clutter.

I cross my fingers as the pile of unsearched boxes becomes smaller, praying that he hasn't thrown them away. He wouldn't. Would he?

He would always say how much he loved my mum's photography, how much she would light up every time she had a camera in her hand. He wouldn't just destroy her life's great joy.

After what has felt like hours of searching, a lens blinks at me as I bring it out into the light for the first time in over a decade.

Surrounding the camera is album after album of photographs. A flurry of emotions hit me as I hug the box tight. A thick cloud of dust leaves an imprint against my shirt.

I search some of the remaining boxes for any other sentimental items and discover another with what looks like more albums in.

I grab them both and make my way out to the entrance of the locker, vowing to come back for the rest one day soon and free her completely from this horrible room.

With a spring back in my step, I exit the building and head out into the crisp October air. As I stand on the sidewalk, getting my bearings, it suddenly dawns on me that I walked here.

It's getting dark and I don't know where I am. There is no way I can carry two boxes all the way back from Manhattan to Brooklyn.

I neatly stack the boxes by the wall and stand over them protectively, before reaching for my phone and debating who to call.

Neither of my friends have cars. New York is such a well-connected city that none of us feel the need to have one and I can't call my father. I sigh, feeling guilty, as I dial the only number I can rely on.

"Hey, Syd! How are you?" Kai's friendly voice bounces down the phone and instantly calms me. A small smile creeps onto my face.

"Syd? You okay?" I let myself listen to his voice, letting his warm tone soothe me for a moment, before snapping back into reality.

"Yeah, yeah, I'm fine, Kai. I just need a favour." The guilt takes over again. I'm always asking Kai for favours.

I know he doesn't mind, but still, it would be nice to do him the favour for a change.

"You need a lift, huh?" I can almost hear him smirking down the phone as I chuckle.

"You guessed it. Can I send you the address?" I can hear Tina in the background, banging pots in the kitchen. I desperately hope I wasn't interrupting them.

"Sure, sure. I'll head out now, Syd." He laughs as he picks his keys up from the table and heads out.

I send him the address and lean back against the wall. I'm so thankful for Kai. I really am.

When I get into his car, he greets me with a smile and doesn't ask questions. I'm grateful for that.

"Home?" he grins. He cranks up the music on his radio and moves his head in time to it.

"Unfortunately." I let out a small laugh and smile back.

Kai knows how I feel about being at home. He doesn't push it further and I'm honestly just happy to sit in his presence. As we drive over the bridge, Kai taps the steering wheel and cracks goofy jokes every time we hit a roadblock to pass the time.

Brooklyn Heights. The sea of brown.

I grumble incoherently as we approach the row of identical townhouses. "Thank you, Kai," I smile. "See you tomorrow."

I grab my precious cargo from his boot and watch him drive away into the distance. I wish I could go with him.

I open and close the front door as softly as I can and head up the stairs to my room, closing the door behind me. I set the boxes down on the floor by my bed and look again at the colour photo that I had set carefully back in the pages of Little Red Riding Hood.

"I'm going to make you proud, mum." I pick up the first box.

I flip through the photo albums, fond memories filling their pages. I vaguely remember taking quite a few of these photos with her. Others I haven't seen before.

I spend an hour looking at the albums, photos of nature, of me and one of her. My mum never enjoyed having her photo taken. In fact, I don't think I have ever seen one. I take the photo out of its sleeve and hug it close. I vow I will get it framed.

One last album is left in the box. I cautiously pick it up and study the cover. It's battered and looks more tired than the others. I'm excited to open it.

I turn the first page. It isn't photos that greet me, however. It's words. Her words. Her journal. I didn't even know she kept a journal.

My stomach churns, as I hold something so private and personal in my hands. I take a deep breath and begin to read.

"I need to get this off my chest…"

6

Eden

March 15

We went to the shop today, Sydney and me. Her eyes lit up as we approached. It made my heart melt.

Sydney loves chatting to my customers and eating the leftover cake when she doesn't think anyone is looking.

I don't mind. The day flew by and we had such a wonderful time.

Sydney asked if we could photograph the fading sky. I said yes. Photography at dusk with my daughter will always be the highlight of my life for as long as I live.

Click.

I stood proudly, watching as she photographed a flower waving gently in the wind.

"Hold the camera steady, Syd." I love teaching her.

She seems to pick it up well. I'm so proud!

Click.

A bird flew across the sky, perfectly highlighted by the fading sun. Sydney's mouth transforms to a straight, thin line as she concentrates, tongue poking out from one side ever so slightly as she takes the shot.

Click.

I capture Sydney, standing in the moonlight. A photograph I will treasure. Always. I hope that she will take her love of the world in all its glory and continue to share that love with all around her.

Time seemed to stand still, even as the light continued to fade around us. This is my favourite time of the day.

Happy with our photographs, Sydney and I call it a night. I hope she knows how talented she is.

March 16

Sydney and I headed to the dark room today. The photos from last night were itching to be developed and I can't wait to add her latest work to the shop.

The dark room is my safe space. It always has been for as long as I can remember. But now, with Sydney by my side, it is so much more than that.

Our dark room is our world - a place where we laugh, cry and make precious memories.

I hope you remember this time in years to come.

March 22

I took Brianna to see Rosa again today. We skipped along the cobbled path to her farmhouse and sung a whole host of silly songs to entertain her.

My little angel has the most gorgeous singing voice. It radiated out for all to hear as the sun started to rise from beneath the hillside. I'm afraid her voice puts mine to shame!

We got to Rosa's early this morning. I have to be back in

time and the sun seems to be at full strength earlier and earlier as the days get brighter and summer approaches.

She was cheery as always, welcoming us in with open arms, as Brianna hurtled her way towards the familiar box of toys in the hallway.

I couldn't stay. But Bri is used to this by now. She is perfectly content with brushing the hair of this weeks favourite teddy bear as I make my way hastily back down the street. I was just in time to kiss Dean goodbye as he made his way to work.

Bri is staying over tonight, a time I know she enjoys, because Rosa spoils her rotten. I miss my little girl though. The house isn't the same without her in it, bouncing all over the place, scattering her few toys wherever she goes.

April 12

It's always important to have a big dream in life. My big dream is to be a photographer. But that dream isn't possible.

So, I content myself with making small contributions to adorn my teashop walls.

To be just content in life is not what I dream for you though, Sydney. I dream that you will do something extraordinary.

My private wish is that you go on and live the life I never could. You become a photographer and you share your talent with the world.

You go out into the light and you show everyone how incredible you are.

But I would never tell you this directly. So, for now, I am at peace with writing it here, surrounded by my innermost thoughts and memories.

Whatever you do, I'll be proud of you, Sydney.

May 16

Dean took Sydney and Brianna to see his parents today. He wasn't best pleased when I said I couldn't go, but I've had to learn to stand up for myself over time, even when it's tough.

I want, no, I need my girls to know that how they live their lives is up to them. So, I try to provide them with the best example of strength I can.

Dean doesn't understand. How could he? I don't blame him. I just want him to know that this isn't my choice, none of it is. But he can't know.

I must be fearless. I've learnt to be fearless. It's getting harder. I always knew that this road would be tough. I always knew that there were other, easier paths. But I also know that it must be this way.

May 28

Sydney knows, better than the rest of my family, what it's like to be an outcast.

She came home crying today and it broke my heart. I wish I could comfort her, tell her my story, give her some hope, but I can't. So we just sat.

We sat together in the dark room and I listened whilst she sobbed. There is no greater heartbreak than watching your child cry.

We turned our minds to developing more pictures, but melancholy sadness still lingered in the air, despite both of us doing what we love.

I wish I could take away your pain, Sydney - more than anything.

June 10

Sydney's bullying is getting worse.

We went out at dusk again to take some more pictures and I told her that I was bullied too - that everything would be okay.

I still didn't tell her why, though. I feel like a coward. My Sydney is brave and open, qualities that I admire so much.

Days like these make it difficult to hide. It's difficult to feel so low and yet fight so hard to preserve what little control I have left over my life.

I know it isn't fair on them and I know they wouldn't judge, but I don't want to be a label, or an abnormality.

I want to be me. Eden Monroe. Nothing more, nothing less.

June 23

Sydney and I watched the sunset together. It was magical.

She looked so content as she snapped the sun fading into the fields surrounding us.

We were bathed in a warm and glorious light. Moments like these are made to be cherished.

I watched as she darted around, trying to find the perfect angle. She is such a natural.

I taught her everything I know about photography, hoping it will be her creative outlet too.

She is already better than I am. She has a gift.

July 12

My writing is my sanctuary. When the world gets tough and all I want to do is scream aloud, I write here.

I'm going to encourage Sydney to write a journal when she's older. I am sure she'd have a far more interesting story to tell than I do.

I hope that she fills the pages of her journal with wonderful memories, happiness, joy.

I hope that it shows her following her dreams, whatever they may be. I hope that she never gives up on her photography.

July 15

Sydney and I were in the darkroom all day today. I could honestly say that this was one of the best days of my life.

We laughed till we cried. We talked about our dreams and hopes for the future.

I told her I hope she will follow her heart wherever it leads her.

"Mamma, I want to be a photographer, just like you," she said, smiling a beautiful, wide, beaming smile.

She thinks I'm a photographer.

If only she knew.

Yet it filled my heart with so much love and hope. She makes my heart whole. She makes me want to dream and then follow through.

She makes me want to be a real photographer, to make her proud, but before I do that, I must be honest.

I must be honest and confide in Dean, Sydney and even little Brianna.

It will be hard. I know it will. But Sydney has taught me that nothing worthwhile in life ever comes easy.

Everything that you love requires you to fight for it. Life needs to be cherished and lived to its full potential.

I have spent most of my life, up to this point, living in fear and even denial.

I hide behind my photographs, hoping that someone will reveal the encrypted message held behind each one. But they don't.

So, I must be brave.

July 18

A travelling art show is coming to the nearby town in a few weeks' time. I really want to go.

This is the first time anything like this has happened so close to home. Maybe I could take Sydney with me?

I believe that everyone should experience art and culture from a young age. Maybe this could be Sydney's chance? It is unlikely to happen here again in our quiet English countryside.

I will surprise her. In a few days' time she finishes school for the summer. I'll tell her then.

She's going to be so excited and I can't wait to experience this with her.

July 20

I took a photo of Sydney today, in perfect colour. Sydney is the colour in my life, the light and everything in between.

She is my everything and deserves to know the truth. So, I need to get this off my chest.

I can't keep this from my family anymore.

I need to tell them.

7

Sydney

I stare at the final few sentences in her journal, thumbing desperately through the remaining pages. But they are all the same. Empty.

My mum was taken before she could find the strength. She was robbed of her one desire to tell us her truth.

I feel angry at the world. She had something to say. Her voice was important. Yet her message for the world faded with her.

I shake my head frantically, unable to comprehend what I have just read. I skim read back through, chasing my thumb over each word. I imagine her writing it.

Did she write it in the darkroom? Or maybe in her bedroom? I don't know. But this journal was important to her.

I continue to read through the passages, again and again. I try to remember each of the exact moments she talks about, remembering some as clear as day, but others are hazier.

I sigh and clutch the book tight against my chest. This old, fading, worn journal has now become my single most prized possession.

A nagging doubt still lingers in the back of my mind. Will I ever find out what was so important she had to tell me?

It's obvious from the journal that my father doesn't know; and my grandparents passed years back, taking any secrets to their graves.

"There must be a way," I whisper to myself, holding the journal tighter. She wrote that I should be determined, that I should never give up.

"I won't give up on you mum." I make a vow to myself in that moment that I will find what she wanted me to know, no matter how long it takes.

* * *

I wake up to find the journal still entangled in my grip. It's my first day back at work since I've been ill and I'm not looking forward to it.

I grab the smartest dress I can find from the rack and get ready in a hurry, thrusting a breakfast bar in my bag as I race out of the door into the waiting car.

"Miss Monroe." The driver nods at me. I force a smile onto my face and nod back. I'm not in the mood for talking this morning. I have too much to think about.

As the car pulls away and crosses the bridge, dread creeps over me once again. I miss the feeling of joy and wonder I felt when crossing the bridge just a day earlier.

This is not me living my best life like mum wanted for me. Am I letting her down? Do I need to rebel? Stand up for myself?

Thoughts whirl round my head as the car continues to speed into Manhattan.

"Here we are, miss," my driver informs.

"Here we are," I mutter darkly under my breath. To say I hate my job is an understatement.

"Sydney, hey!" Kai bounds over to me, smiling broadly.

Kai is the only person I like in this stupid office. My colleagues are all executive wannabes. I know for a fact that the only reason they speak to me is because I'm the Dean's daughter.

"Hey, Kai." I glare at a picture of Dean Monroe grinning from the wall. He never smiles at me.

I need not feign enthusiasm around him. He knows how I feel.

"What's up with old Deano? He's been in a proper foul mood all morning."

"My father is always in a foul mood, Kai. You should be used to it by now." A conversation about my father is the last thing I want right now.

Kai and I head toward our offices. He is telling me some story about how he cooked dinner for Tina and she swears he gave her food poisoning, while I pretend to listen.

I usually love listening to Kai's stories. He tells them with such depth and animation. Today, however, I just want to get lost in my own thoughts.

"Right, Syd. I have today's schedule for you here. Looks standard." He hands the paper to me, a knowing smirk on his face.

"Wait, isn't that Noah's job? You are head of finance, why are you getting my schedules?" He grins at me. "I know how much you hate Noah and everyone else in this place."

"Oh and I added lunch with me to your ever so busy schedule." I roll my eyes and wave him away. I always eat lunch with Kai and he knows it. I still think it is sweet that he took the time to add it to my schedule.

The world of real estate is never appealing, but today, with so much running round my mind, it is beyond unbearable.

I think about my mum's journal, going over every single detail in my head. My heart aches as I think of all the opportunities I missed with her.

We never got to go to that art show. She never even got to surprise me with the tickets like she planned. Life is so cruel.

I rest my forehead against my desk. Maybe reading her journal wasn't such a good idea. Maybe dad is right and I should bury my head in the sand just like he does.

That isn't me though. My mum always commended me for being so open and honest about my feelings.

"Express yourself, baby," she used to say. "Don't hide away."

"I don't want to let you down, mum." I lean back in the chair before jumping up to someone crashing through the door.

"Gosh, Kai. You never do anything quietly! What do you want?" He pouts at me and points dramatically at the clock on my wall.

I groan. I have just spent the entire morning lost inside my head, without getting a single task done. I heave myself up from my desk and head out with Kai for lunch, even though I should really stay to catch up on this morning's workload.

Kai and I decide to treat ourselves to bagels. I don't know who we are trying to kid. We get them every day, from the same little café on the corner.

"So, how's Tina?" I ask, as Kai shoves a bit of bagel into his mouth.

He deliberates this question as he chews, before grimacing.

"I think she's still mad about the food poisoning incident."

Tina is Kai's wife and is the nicest lady I've met in New York. They got married last year and I was her bridesmaid. Kai is completely and utterly devoted to her; I can tell from the way he speaks. A small grin starts from the corners of his mouth and continues to grow the more he talks.

I wonder if my mum and dad were ever that devoted to each other? They never showed affection publicly, not like Kai and Tina.

Kai is a bit younger than my father and yet he doesn't treat me like someone beneath him. He treats me as a friend. An equal. That's what I love about Kai.

"Hello? Sydney! Are you in there?" he laughs. I am pulled jerkily from my trance by Kai waving his hand in front of my face.

"You know I love bagels, but I've never gone into a trance over one. Maybe we should call the tabloids?" He winks at me and continues to eat. I glare at him and slap his arm playfully.

"Hey Syd, I meant to tell you something. You know you used to love photography?" I pause. I don't remember telling Kai that, but now I wish that whenever I did, I hadn't. I'm not ready to explain why I don't photograph anymore. Not even to him.

"Yeah?" I reply cautiously, not wanting him to continue.

"Well, there's some exhibition on in Brooklyn coming up. Some guy at work was on about it earlier. I thought I'd let you know."

My heart sinks. "An exhibition?"

"Yeah, it sounds cool! It's all vintage, you know, paintings, photography, whatever."

I smile at him weakly and nod. The old me would have

jumped at the opportunity to go to an exhibition. Especially one showcasing vintage art, but that was my mum's dream.

She dreamed that she would take me to my first exhibition. Now she's not here. It wouldn't feel right.

"Send me the information. I'll look," I eventually reply.

I know it isn't wise to take the details of this event, but I can't help myself. I tell myself that it is just so Kai doesn't ask questions. But is that really the reason? I do not think it is.

8

Freddie

Ping.

I hold my breath. I really don't want to redo this proposal. As I open Lucas's email, I feel my heart racing.

"Please like it," I beg the screen.

I skim through the email and sigh in relief. "Project brief accepted."

Now all that is left is to go to this stupid event. It's in one weeks time and I am dreading it. It gets closer with every tick of the clock, its constant noise goading me.

Satisfied with my work, I head out early. I keep my head down as I duck out of the doors onto the street. I am ashamed to say that I have been blatantly ignoring Mason. I know it is my fault for saying I would go out with him at some point, but still.

I only slow my pace when I am convinced that I'm far enough away from the office block. I debate whether I should go home. The answer is a resounding no.

Ever since the run in with my father, I have been avoiding

that place like the plague. I know mom must miss me. I miss her too and I hate leaving her alone with him. But I don't have a choice.

She won't leave him, that's her decision. I won't be near him or that flat. That's mine.

I wish things were different, more than anything, but I can't help but feel betrayed. She must see how miserable it makes me, even if I try my best to keep it hidden. She must know that he's tearing us both apart.

I continue along the street, deep in thought, not knowing where my feet are taking me. Before I even have the chance to comprehend, I am standing in front of it.

My favourite mural on the highline.

I exhale. There's something about modern art, with all its colours and vibrancy that makes me feel calm. This mural is beautiful. Its colours stand out brilliantly against the whitewash of the wall and it instantly brings a smile to my face.

I wish I could make art full time. That is my biggest wish, but ever since my father went off the rails, my dreams have escaped me.

The constant reminders of how tough reality is always brings me back to earth. I don't dream anymore, not really. I just survive. That's what it feels like, anyway. I wake up. I go to work. I go to sleep. That is the basic outline of my day. That's not living. It's existing.

I miss the days when I would look up at the sky and tell the stars my wishes, the days when I was naïve enough to believe that love is all we need. I don't believe that anymore. My mother and father said they loved each other once and my grandparents before them. Love never ends well. It's never enough.

I continue to explore the mural, my eyes covering every single inch, so I don't miss a single detail.

Leaning back against the wall opposite the mural, I allow my gaze to shift back down to the tarmac in defeat. I come here to find hope and inspiration, but today I'm just not feeling it.

What if there is no hope left to find? What if this is as good as it gets? I try to remain calm, as my brain races along at a hundred miles an hour.

I turn away from the mural with a heavy heart. This isn't the experience I wanted. I wanted to find hope, something to cling onto, instead I just made myself feel a lot worse.

"What is wrong with me? Why do I always have to screw everything up?" I kick at the ground in frustration as I make my way back to the flat.

I feel my pace getting slower as I near my street. "The sooner I move out of this dump the better," I murmur darkly as I approach the flat. I grab supplies from the kitchen as I pass through and head straight to my bedroom.

There is no way I am going out there again if he comes in screaming and yelling. I bolt my door and slump down onto the mattress in the corner.

I think about mom. At this moment she is probably changing a bed or scrubbing at stains on the floor. She never complains. Even when all her wages follow dad out the door and into the local bar. I don't know how she does it.

She works all hours of the day, with three cleaning jobs on the go, just to keep us in rent and basic food. She puts up with so much.

Hatred for my father swells over me once again. This is a regular occurrence when I'm here, alone, lost in my thoughts.

It always starts with me thinking about my mother, slaving away just to keep the family afloat. Then it moves across to the man who did this to us and anger boils over me.

I help where I can, but mom doesn't like to take money from me. She knows I'm saving to move out of here.

The times I have tried to give her money have always been when dad has blown her wages on bets and alcohol. But it is always returned unspent, in an envelope marked with a small heart, pushed under my door.

I don't know how she got the money those times we really struggled. But she did. And I'm so grateful to her.

I like to think that one day this will all be over. I like to think she will leave him and we'll move. Somewhere far away. Somewhere quiet. We'd be so happy, just like we used to be. But she won't leave him. Not when she blames herself for his actions.

I often wonder if dad knows what he is doing to us. Does he sit there in the bar and get drunk to chase away the pain? Or is he just being a jerk?

I don't know the answer, but I wish I did...

* * *

"Grant. What are you doing?" My mom screams.

"Stop it! This is all we have!" She is sobbing now, clawing at my father, desperately trying to get him to stop.

I just hide, like the coward I am.

My mom is looking around the room, desperately, as if searching for something, until her eyes lock onto mine and she exhales in relief.

"Grant," she tries again, "We can talk about this outside.

You're scaring Freddie."

I retreat into my room, grab a blanket and huddle into the furthest corner of my bare mattress.

Thud.

Everything goes quiet as I let out a small whimper.

The door slams.

I get up and cautiously move to the door.

My mom is on the floor, huddled into a ball and crying, but I can't get my feet to move towards her.

I just stand there, like a complete idiot, while she cries alone into her hands.

A thought comes into my small ten-year-old brain and I smile to myself, before tiptoeing back into my dark room.

"This always makes me feel better. I want mom to feel better too." I grab it from the bed and head back to where my mom is still sobbing in a ball.

"Mom?" I ask quietly, shaking her gently by the shoulder.

"Oh, gosh, Freddie. You shouldn't be seeing me like this. You shouldn't have seen any of that." She frantically wipes at her eyes and tries to smile.

"It's ok mom, I just brought you this."

I swear I see her heart break in that moment as she smiles at me through the fresh flow of tears cascading down her face.

"Your teddy? But you can't sleep without him Fred." She smiles reassuringly at me.

I push my bear towards her. "He's yours now momma. You can't sleep either. I hear you."

She takes him in her arms and squeezes him tight against her chest. "I'll take good care of him, darling and one day I'll buy you an entire box of bears, I promise."

I smile at this thought, completely oblivious to the fact that we don't have the money to afford just one bear, let alone a whole box.

"His name is Bentley." I murmur proudly. "He'll look after you, mom."

She gets up slowly from her ball on the floor and smiles again.

"I'll look after him too, Fred." She hugs my bear again and starts to walk to her room. It is late by now and way past my bedtime.

"Night, Freddie." She smiles at me, blowing a kiss, as I clumsily pretend to catch it.

As her door closes, I whisper into the wood. "Night, momma. I hope Bentley helps you sleep better."

I blow her another kiss, hoping she catches it, before heading back to bed.

I lie awake for ages without Bentley. I haven't slept without him since I was born. My arms feel empty and a single tear drops down my face, but it's worth it.

Mom isn't moving. She isn't crying. She's asleep. For the first time in months.

* * *

I wake up with a start, tears freely flowing down my cheeks. I switch the lamp on and breathe slowly.

Midnight. Mom should be home soon.

I get up slowly, checking every so often to see whether I could hear any noise. But the flat is silent. Empty.

I tiptoe into my parent's bedroom, moving round the mattress to my mom's side. Not that he is ever here to sleep next to his wife anyway.

I know exactly what I am looking for. Bentley.

He is tucked up under the sheets and my heart surges. Mom still sleeps with him. She still has him. And he still comforts her.

I remember sleeping so restlessly for weeks after I gave Bentley to my mom. But seeing him here now, tucked up in her bed, makes all that worth it.

"Thank you for looking after her." Fresh tears rush down my face as I stroke Bentley's fur.

I blow a kiss, aiming directly to her pillow. I hope she feels its presence when she gets home. I hope she knows how much I love her.

9

Sydney

Ping.

An email hurtles loudly into my inbox, disturbing my peace. It's from Kai. I should have known. He never goes back on his promises. He promised me information about the exhibition and here it is.

The title taunts me from the screen.

"The Brooklyn Art Exhibition. Join us for a day exploring all aspects of vintage artwork and meet the artists! From paintings to photography, this exhibition has it all!"

"You would have loved this mum." I look through the portfolio of images cluttering the screen.

Ring. Ring.

I stare at my phone and a grin creeps across my face. Valentina, one of my two closest friends. I haven't heard from her or Alessia in ages, so a phone call is long overdue.

As soon as I pick up the phone, words tumble out of Valentina's mouth and tangle incoherently into the air.

"Woah. Val! Slow down!" I laugh at her chaos.

"Sorry, sorry! I'm just so excited, but also super bummed at the same time!" I chuckle again. Val trying to say something calmly when she is in this excitable state is near enough impossible.

"They're going to feature my painting! At the exhibition! Oh, you must have heard of it. Have you heard of it?" As I listen to the words pouring out of her, I feel my shoulders droop.

"Why is everyone talking about this stupid exhibition?"

She doesn't give me a chance to break my trance and reply before she begins again.

"Well, anyway, it's a super big deal and I'm so excited. But I can't go because mom needs me to clear the things from my old room on that day and she won't let me swap days."

I'm still in a daze at this point as her words continue to hit me. Why can't I get a break?

"It is so unfair! So, I need a massive favour, Syd. I need you to go to the exhibition for me. And talk to people on my behalf."

Wait... What?

What did she just day?

"Syd?"

"Sydney?"

She is excitedly yelling down the phone at me, making me jump, as her voice suddenly registered in my brain.

"Sorry, what?"

"You'll go to the exhibition for me, won't you, Syd? This could be a huge deal for me." Desperation creeps into her voice She is right. This exhibition could propel her career.

What sort of friend would I be if I didn't help her out?

"How would I know what to say, Val?" I ask, but by this

point, I know she has defeated me.

My conscience has won.

"I will write every single question and answer I can think of down for you and keep my phone on all day for last-minute questions. Oh and I'll also send you the description of the painting, so you know the inspiration."

I start to let out a sigh, but cover my mouth quickly to stop it. Val may be eccentric, but she would never make me do anything I wasn't comfortable with. I cannot let her lose this opportunity because of me.

"I'll do it, Val." I put on my most cheery tone and smile as she squeals in excitement.

"Thank you so much! I need to get ready. There is less than a week to prepare! I'll send you an email as soon as I can!" She cuts off the phone just as the last word leaves her mouth. She seems so excited and I laugh at her enthusiasm. I wish I had something I was this enthusiastic about.

I used to have a fire within me burning in search of my dreams. A dream to be a photographer. But that flame has long since been extinguished.

Now I work in real estate. As an assistant. This is not what she hoped for me, but I don't dare to dream anymore. Dreams don't come true. At least not for me.

* * *

The days fly by in the lead up to the exhibition and before I know it, it is just two days away.

Valentina hasn't stopped. She rings me at least three times a day to check everything is okay.

I feel sorry for her. Her first big exhibition and she can't even go. Why does her mom have to ruin everything for her?

Valentina moved out from her parents house just over two years ago. She craved freedom and felt trapped, so one day she just left. To their credit, her parents give her an allowance, although it is tiny compared to what they earn.

She seems happy though and I am thrilled she gets to follow her dreams. She now lives in a beautiful Brooklyn apartment, in a diverse cultural neighbourhood and has everything set up for her own personal art studio.

Why can't she reschedule her parents and go to the exhibition? I have no idea. Val doesn't really talk much about her family. All I know is that she muttered something about her parents moving to a new house and needing the room cleared.

My guess would be that they threatened Val with cutting her allowance if she refused. Just like they always do.

I try to concentrate on the latest email she has sent me. I start to read, highlighting areas that seem important as I go. My brain aches. I know nothing about paintings and I really don't want to let her down.

I head to the printer and print every page off, hoping that pages in my hands might make more sense. It's a long shot.

Dad will not be happy about the amount of ink I am using. However, this vague thought is only fleeting as I ponder how much money he has to replace it and where he got that money from. Dirty money from the sale of mum's shop and our family home.

I lost all ties to the UK one month after mum passed away. He had announced the move to New York just two weeks after she died. I will never forgive him for that.

As the last pages churn through the printer, I spot Kai standing and chatting to a colleague. I wish I had his confidence.

I wish I could get lost for a while. Instead, I duck into the corner of the copy room, hoping he doesn't spot me on his way through.

I breathe a sigh of relief as he wanders past, coffee in hand and a stack of papers wedged precariously under his arm. He is still chatting with the same colleague, laughing together as they walk.

I don't like letting people into my life. Even if they are only colleagues stopping for a chat. The more people you let in, the more risk you have of getting hurt. I can't get hurt again.

I have a small inner circle: Kai, Valentina and Alessia. I tell them everything – well, almost everything. Truth is, I haven't told my full story to anyone. I haven't wanted to.

The minute those words would come out of my mouth, the truth would become my reality. I am comfortable living with the denial. I know this isn't healthy, but it's just how I am.

As soon as my family stopped talking and showing emotion, I closed my life up. I built walls. And I shut them around me.

My family is not in my inner circle. We don't talk to each other anymore. We don't show emotion. In fact, I would say emotion is discouraged. Brianna is wild and out at parties most weekends. My father is a workaholic. Either way, I never see them. Our family is out of control.

When mum was alive, showing emotions was to be encouraged. We would always talk together in the darkroom, just the two of us, as we processed our pictures. I miss the times that I could be an open book.

The printer bleeps at me and the reminiscing ceases. I grab my papers, rush back to my office and study them.

* * *

It is the day of the exhibition and I am feeling more and more nervous. Valentina's future literally rests in my hands and that is an immense responsibility.

A whole number of things could go wrong. I could mess up and not impress people that could potentially transform her life and career.

I could freak out and break down at the sight of the exact style of art my mum used to love – the art I used to love.

I scroll through the photos on my laptop, trying desperately to prepare myself, but as my mum used to tell me: "Art is a feeling that has to be experienced."

You don't get that same feeling, that same energy, from staring at a computer screen. There is nothing I can do to prepare. I know this will be overwhelming.

"What do you think, mum? This is what you wanted for us. To experience an exhibition." I know she will be with me today, her heart bursting with pride, as she watches me surrounded by styles she loved.

"Embrace it, Sydney." I know that is what she would say.

My steps feel heavy as I walk through Brooklyn's streets. I still have plenty of time, but I want to be prepared and they allow creators in before the public. I want to experience it before the rush.

I am here to do Valentina proud. I am here to make myself proud and you, mum.

"I know I can do it. I am strong. I am." I push through the double doors and into a massive room filled floor to ceiling with art.

10

Freddie

Equipped with my phone, a notebook and a small digital camera, I head across the bridge and into Brooklyn.

I've been to Brooklyn many times, but today feels different. I'm still not looking forward to this exhibition. The pay check at the end, however, is a different world entirely.

That may sound sad to some. Hell, it sounds sad to me. But I really do just work pay check to pay check.

I walk through Brooklyn Heights and gaze at the brown townhouses stretching ahead of me. I can't help but feel jealous.

How come some people get to live in houses like these with big sloping steps and bay windows, while others live in dingy flats with bare mattresses and creaky floorboards?

I watch as a young woman ahead of me emerges flustered out of the door, grabbing at a bag as she goes.

Our eyes lock, just for a second and I swear I see her contort with sadness, although she doesn't stop long enough for me to get more than a fleeting glance.

I watch as she disappears down the street and into the distance.

I shake the feeling of pity from my mind and tell myself that she is probably just like all the other rich girls on this street, crying over a handbag.

Rich people like the ones on this street do not know what it is like to experience genuine problems. Problems like not being able to afford rent, or not knowing where your next meal is coming from.

I continue my journey through Brooklyn, pushing all thoughts of the social system out of my mind before it makes me even more irritable.

The exhibition is in a diverse neighbourhood. I feel instantly more at home here. There are beautiful murals littering the walls and the houses are messy and imperfect.

I love it.

This street is in the same borough as the Brooklyn Heights showrooms and yet it feels like a whole other world.

The street continues to uplift me as I walk the last stretch to the exhibition hall.

I push through the double doors and into a massive room filled floor to ceiling with art.

The disappointment immediately hits me.

Coming from all the colour and diversity of the roads surrounding the venue, this is a massive let down. I hate vintage art.

Pieces adorn the room, yet not one of them has a splash of colour. In fact, nothing has colour. Everything is in black and white, or sepia.

"This is just as bad as I thought it was going to be," I grumble to myself loudly.

"You obviously have a very low opinion of art and beauty then."

I jump and spin around, almost losing my balance. I didn't think anyone was around and yet here I am - offending someone within the first thirty seconds of arrival.

I turn to face the voice and register that she looks just as shocked as I do at being caught. She stares down at the floor, her hair falling messily around her face. I guess she hates confrontation as much as I do.

I remember why I am here and offer her a small smile. I am here to make a good impression, to get a good story, neither of which will happen if I go upsetting anyone.

"Sorry, I didn't mean to offend anyone." I offer a wider smile.

Staring thoughtfully, she takes a while contemplating an answer. I stand awkwardly.

"That's okay. I wasn't sure I was going to like it either." She speaks quietly, almost too soft to register each delicate syllable that falls from her mouth, as she continues to deliberate over her word choice.

"Maybe just give it a chance, yeah? It might surprise you." Her cheeks flush as she smiles and turns to walk away.

"Wait!" I call after her. "I didn't get your name." She turns back to face me, surprised. It is obvious she is not used to making conversation with strangers.

"Sydney. Sydney Monroe," she whispers, before walking away to a stand at the far corner of the room.

I watch her go as I try to comprehend what had just happened. She had a funny mix of accents. I would say mostly British, but with a hint of New Yorker. Intriguing.

"Freddie Robinson?" I jump at a voice from behind me,

quickly turning to look away from her, breaking our gaze.

An old man is standing behind me with a clipboard.

"Press meeting starts in five minutes, after that you can walk around the venue, take your pictures, conduct your interviews…" He waffles on like this for a couple of minutes as I space out.

"I've only just met her. This is ridiculous." I keep repeating this to myself, but my brain doesn't seem to care. My brain wants to see her again.

"No. You want to see her again. Admit it." My subconscious butts in, waging a war against my common sense.

By the time clipboard man has finished speaking at me, I have missed ninety-five percent of his speech. I nod politely and head over to the press corner, hoping I can stay focused long enough to do my job.

The meeting lasts longer than I expected and even by the end of it I am still not convinced about this art form. But I am going to give it a chance.

As we head out of the side office, journalists jostle, figuring out the best pieces for their respective stories. That is what I should do too, but I don't. Instead, I look back over to where Sydney's stall is positioned and notice her talking to a woman, presumably about the artwork behind her head.

"So, Sydney is a painter?" She doesn't look like a painter.

I pace for a while, trying to pluck up the courage to talk to her. I'm a journalist. Talking to people is my job. So why is this so hard?

My face flushes a shade of red I didn't know existed as her gaze locks onto mine.

Wait.

My mind flickers back to this morning, walking through

58

Brooklyn Heights.

It's her.

The woman racing flustered down the steps of a perfectly kept townhouse. The woman who glanced at me with such sadness in her eyes.

What is she doing here?

I know the sorts of people that live in those townhouses and they are not the sort to visit and display at an exhibition.

She is still staring at me. I'm still staring at her, continuing to pace. I curse myself for looking like such an idiot in front of her.

What must she think of me?

A pacing beetroot staring at her from across the room is the definition of creepy.

"Snap out of it, Freddie. You don't make friends. You don't even talk to strangers. You do not want to talk to her." The pep talk doesn't work though and soon enough my feet are taking me towards her, step by step.

"I'm Freddie."

She looks at me, confused.

What a mug.

I didn't even say hello first. What must she think? I try desperately to conjure something remotely sensible to say next, but words fail me. I feel so stupid.

"You're a journalist. Right, Freddie?"

She lets out a small laugh and immediately puts me at ease.

"Confession?"

She is clearly amused by how much this is affecting me, even more so when the only response I can muster is to gulp and nod.

"I'm not actually the artist. My friend, Valentina, couldn't be here today. So, I'm helping her out and displaying her piece."

I stare at her again. So, she isn't an artist?

"Hello? Freddie? Are you going to write this down?"

Damn it. She thinks I am recording an interview, when all I wanted was to talk to her.

"I – um. I'm sorry I need to go." It's the only reply I can muster, as I rush away from her table.

I search the room and photograph some of the artwork on display, not trusting myself to talk to anyone.

Never in my life have I been this much of an idiot, especially not in front of a girl - a girl that lives in Brooklyn Heights, for goodness sake.

Whizzing around the exhibition room, trying to forget Sydney Monroe, I interview people as quickly as I can. There is nothing I want more than to get out of here. Away from her. She is driving me crazy.

I hurriedly finish my work, before fleeing out of the door and out into the cool October air, collapsing down onto a step and pulling the excess material of my jumper tight around my shivering body.

11

Sydney

I watch as he rushes around the room, taking photographs and conducting interviews. He looks uncomfortable, embarrassed even. He looks how I feel.

Over the years, one of my talents has been masking my feelings - remaining calm and collected on the outside, screaming internally. That's how I feel right now.

I can't believe I spoke to another human I didn't have a previous connection with. I can't believe it felt as natural as it did.

He must feel the same as I do, but judging by his reaction, I'm guessing remaining calm isn't one of his talents. I am proud of myself though and I know mum would be too.

I spoke to him. I was confident.

Maybe coming to this exhibition was a good idea after all? Maybe this is the start of a new me?

I'm distracted from those thoughts by the sight of Freddie practically hurling himself out of the double doors we both came through.

"What am I doing?" I follow him out.

He's sitting on the step, huddled over, hands thrust deep into pockets, lost in thought.

"Hey, Freddie?" I sit down next to him and he turns to me in complete shock.

"What are you doing here?" There is a guarded edge to his voice now that wasn't there before.

It shocks me. Maybe he's better at masking his feelings than I thought.

"You never got to finish your interview." I keep my voice light, hoping to put him at ease.

I see his shoulders relax, almost as if on reflex. As soon as he catches himself however, he tenses back up.

What made him like this? I instantly feel sad for the stranger sitting beside me.

"I got all the interviews I need," he replies gruffly, keeping his eyes averted from mine.

Something about him makes me feel brave. He's hurting, just like I am. He's intriguing.

"Coffee?" I ask, before I really understand what I'm saying.

His head snaps round and his eyes meet mine. They are wide and unsure. "What did you just say?"

I'm hesitant now, a little startled at his reaction. "Did you want to get coffee?" I stumble over my words, before adding, "With me?"

I have never done this. I have never asked anyone who isn't in my inner circle to spend time with me.

His face flushes with confusion and for a moment I swear I see pain fly through his eyes.

"Why would I want to do that?" he mutters, his voice trying to come across as harsh.

It doesn't. His voice breaks at the last word.

It doesn't matter though. I don't know how to answer the question for him. Why would he want to get coffee with me? We don't know each other.

So, I avert my eyes and reply quietly, "I don't know."

He looks confused at this answer, as if he was expecting me to say something different. He tries to meet my eyes, but I don't let him. I am far too embarrassed. I never get involved with making friends anymore, this is the reason. I've been burnt too many times.

"Okay," I whisper and get up to go back into the exhibition.

Part of me wants him to jump up and tell me he would love to get a coffee with me.

Instead, he sits there, head down, hands knotted in his lap.

I slouch back to the exhibition doors, still clinging onto the hope that he'll call me back, but he doesn't make a sound. So, I push through the double doors and navigate through the sea of people, accepting the fact that he doesn't want to know me.

12

Freddie

I let her walk away. I instantly feel the powerful waves of regret as I hear the door slam shut behind her. She was just trying to be nice and I treat her like dirt. This feels like it may have just been the single biggest mistake of my life.

I try to shake the memory of her, to no avail. The scent of her perfume still lingers in the cold air. Her voice is still ringing in my ears. And her smile is all I see.

That smile.

No one has ever smiled at me like that. Yet she seemed so unsure, almost a little afraid. The hurt was clearly visible in her eyes.

I cannot even deal with my own pain, let alone someone else's. But it doesn't stop me from wanting to try to take hers away.

I consider going back in, apologising and asking if the offer still stands. But pride gets in my way and instead, I express myself in one of the few ways I know how.

I retrace my steps, walking away from the exhibition, walking away from Sydney.

I turn around every five seconds, while the door is still in view, hoping that Sydney will appear and come after me, before losing hope and continuing my walk, quickening the pace to keep myself warm.

Even the artwork cluttering the walls around me cannot compete with the image of her racing around my brain.

As I reach her road, a war of judgement rages on inside my head. Poor judgement inevitably wins out, as I push my feelings into the hands of destiny.

Who knows, maybe this will be the best decision I ever make?

I doubt it, but I can hope.

I race now, feet pounding towards the bridge and across to Manhattan. Hope fills my body and it carries me. I have never been so desperate to get to work in all my life.

As I burst through the office doors, Mason stares at me open-mouthed. I don't stop to talk to him though. I can't stop.

I will not let these thoughts, these feelings, running around my head fade away. I pull up a blank document and write, my mind whirring, as I do my best to recall every word.

I never liked vintage art. I thought that colour would always prevail. My shallow mind thought that colour brought the beauty.

I was so wrong.

The passion brings the beauty. Someone told me to give vintage art a try and so I did. I'm glad I did.

In a world of so much colour, busyness and chaos, it is nice to see a stripped back version of reality. Everyone has a distinct reality. She helped me to understand that.

As I looked around the exhibition hall, at first I saw dark, lifeless works, but then I blinked.

I looked again. I saw hope and feeling. People's lives embodied into the paper, each one with its own special meaning. Each piece stands out for a reason and each reason is completely unique. Every art piece is unique.

You may be tempted to say that black and white art is boring, that it has no depth. I beg you to visit an exhibition, just like the one I visited today. Go with an open mind and embrace every little detail you see.

Speak to the artists. Hear their story. Absorb every word they utter.

You will fall in love. I can promise you that...

I pause and lean back in my chair, before pulling out my camera. She's there, smiling at someone in the foreground, speaking in earnest about the painting behind her.

She says she knows nothing about art, that she is just helping a friend. I beg to differ. No one can fake that kind of passion.

She sparkles from the inside out, without even knowing it. Whatever it is, she is fighting it and she shouldn't.

It is obvious how much she loves vintage art, but something is holding her back. I want to know what that thing is. I want to help her.

I go back to filling my mind with hope as I continue to write my article. I hope she finds her way back to me.

Slam.

"Freddie. What are you doing? Why aren't you at the exhibition?" Lucas crashes through the door, a thunder cloud radiating around him, as he begins to rage.

"I found all the inspiration I needed." I stutter, trying to remain confident, despite knowing that he could fire me if he got cross or didn't like what he saw.

"Fine. Make sure you hit the deadline and make sure I'll like it. Else you're in trouble." He narrows his eyes at me, before stalking back out of the room, closing the door firmly.

I try to block out Lucas's words as I huddle back over my laptop, focusing my energies to how I felt seeing Sydney so passionate about the art she was displaying.

I channel this desire into my own writing, using her energy to supplement my own and by the time the clock reaches seven, I already have a first draft written.

I think this is the fastest I have ever written a draft. I'm impressed with myself and it's all thanks to Sydney.

I look at the clock and then down to my phone. She'd be home by now. Wouldn't she? I pull my coat tight around my body and try my best to focus on remaining hopeful, as I gather up my things and head out into the darkness of the city.

By the time I go to bed, it is nearly midnight. I glance at my phone just one more time, before throwing it across the room.

I have well and truly messed this up.

Feeling frustrated, I hit my head against the pillow, although the chance of me getting any sleep is slim.

I get up and grab my phone from its sorry position on the floor, checking it one more time.

Nothing.

I gently place it beside me and try to sleep.

I must get to work early tomorrow for a team meeting. Lucas is annoyed at me already. My mind needs to be sharp.

Despite all my best efforts however, I can't seem to drift off. Sydney still clutters my mind, no matter how much I try to forget her.

How can someone I have only just met have such an impact on me?

I really don't understand.

Ping.

My phone vibrates, as several new messages come through. I grab my phone and stare at the screen.

My heart stops. Disappointment surges.

13

Sydney

I walk home, disappointment guiding my every step. The first person I had felt able to let in had vanished out of my life just as quickly as he arrived.

The exhibition was a success. Val will be thrilled when I tell her. I don't feel like celebrating though. I'm proud of myself for coping, but I can't stop thinking about Freddie.

He's in pain and I can't do anything to take that feeling away from him. If I could, I would, although I have no idea why. I barely know him.

My heart feels heavy as I walk the streets towards my home. I keep expecting him to be there - sitting on a doorstep or standing under a tree, waiting for me. It's that small piece of hope that keeps my feet moving forwards, eyes always searching.

Several times I think I see him, waiting to cross the road, or going up the steps to an apartment. It never is, though and as I reach my house, the disappointment surges through me once more.

I know he would never wait for me, but all the while I was walking there was hope. Now there is none. He's gone. He has disappeared into this vast city and I will never see him again.

I open the door and pray Brianna is out. I really don't want to talk to her tonight. Trudging up the stairs, I feel completely and utterly defeated.

"Sydney!"

I spin around in annoyance. Brianna is sitting on her chair swinging her legs, waving a piece of paper at me.

"What?" I snap. I'm seriously not in the mood to hear whatever she is about to tell me.

"Jeez, what's wrong with you? You have mail, that's all." She rolls her eyes at me sarcastically and hands me the paper.

"You're welcome," she calls, but I don't hear her. I slam my door shut, looking down at the paper in my hands.

There is no address, only Sydney, scrawled across the front.

I shake my head, not even allowing myself to hope. I cannot take anymore disappointment, not today.

The envelope is sealed tight and inside I am greeted by a sea of lined paper.

A letter.

I hold my breath as I unfold the delicately placed note and read the name at the bottom.

"Freddie."

14

Freddie

Sydney,

I know that this will come as a shock to you and I will explain, I promise, but first let me tell you how sorry I am.

I should never have let you walk away. It was rude of me. I just didn't know how to react. I know that isn't an excuse. I'm not trying to excuse my behaviour. I just want you to know the truth.

Today at the exhibition wasn't the first time I saw you. It wasn't the first time our eyes met.

I saw you this morning, outside your house. You looked flustered as you stumbled out of the building, but even under all the chaos there was a hint of sadness in your eyes. Our eyes only met for a second before you headed off and I hate to say it, but I judged you. I judged you for where you lived and I'm not proud of myself Sydney. Really, I'm not.

From the very first time I saw you, something intrigued me and then there you were. Standing behind me at the exhibition.

Call it fate, call it destiny, whatever you want. I was happy.

I only really acknowledged I had seen you before when you walked away.

Thoughts went crazy in my mind and I went a little insane trying to pluck up the courage to talk to you.

I was an idiot, Sydney.

I walked away from you so many times. Each time I regretted it more than the last.

This probably sounds crazy and I wouldn't blame you if you wanted a restraining order after this letter, but I just had to try. And this was the only way I could think to contact you. I had to tell you how I felt when I saw you, why I was so rude.

I felt an instant connection, a connection I never thought possible to feel.

Maybe you felt it too. I don't know.

What I do know is that I couldn't let you go without trying one last time.

I have never bothered with friends before and I'm not saying we will become friends.

I am volatile, but I want to get to know you. Even if it's just for an hour and then we never talk again.

It is better to try and fail than to never try at all. My mom always used to tell me that.

So, if you want to meet me, I will be in the Urban Vintage café, Brooklyn at four on Friday.

If you need an address, you can text me.

I completely understand if you don't want to come, but I'll be there and I hope you are too.

Freddie.

15

Sydney

I stare at the letter in my hands, re-reading it over and over, finding some comfort from his feelings poured out over the page. Should I go? That would be stupid. Wouldn't it?

"What should I do, mum?" I look up at my ceiling and then around the room. He sounds so sincere, but then again do I need this kind of pressure in my life?

Freddie didn't even seem sure whether this would lead to a friendship. I could go and he could hurt me. We could chat and I could enjoy myself. Then he could get up and walk away. I don't think I could take that. I can't cope with people leaving me.

Or what if I hurt him? What if I decide it is too much and I get up and leave? I don't want to cause him any pain. Then again, what if this is the start of something incredible?

"Two broken pieces don't make a whole, Sydney." What ifs circle around my brain, driving me crazy for what seems like hours. I try to convince myself of all the reasons not to go, but his letter has done something to me.

Maybe it is time to follow my heart and not my head for a change. Just like mum did.

I fall asleep to these feelings whirring around, waking up every few hours with new possibilities clamouring for attention. Thank goodness I have a day off tomorrow.

The sunlight streaming through my window is enough to start my morning with a smile. I go for a walk, despite the chilly October air nipping around me, as I huddle into my winter coat.

Three days until Friday. Three days to decide.

I don't know where my legs are taking me, but I trust and let them lead until they reach the bridge.

I smile and sit down on the nearest bench, watching the passers-by. This feels like no-man's-land, crossing between the Boroughs: one end Brooklyn, the other Manhattan. We are so connected and yet so far apart.

I wonder where Freddie lives. Either way, this bridge connects me to him. This bridge also symbolises freedom. If I wanted to, I could cross to Manhattan and just get lost.

I could leave dad and his cold nature behind and make my own way. I could have a fresh start, but that isn't an option for me right now.

So, in a way, this bridge is mocking me, calling me over when it knows full well I can't. Bri needs her sister. My father can't be trusted to take care of her. He doesn't even acknowledge her most of the time. So, the duty falls to me, keeping me trapped in Brooklyn, surrounded by memories that haunt me and eleven lost years.

I look across to the Manhattan skyline. It is all so unknown I went to Manhattan for college. I go for work and I went to the storage locker. That is it. There is so much of New York have yet to experience, so much I don't know exists.

I know I could explore if I wanted to, but I'm afraid. I'm afraid that I'll go and not want to come back. I'm not brave enough.

So, I stay at the Brooklyn end of the bridge, looking wistfully at the passers-by. I follow my head, not my heart. One day I'll surrender to my heart. I must hold on to that thought.

I watch as a group of tourists reach the Brooklyn and leap excitedly. Their cameras are clicking, taking photos of each other and the surrounding scenery.

I feel a pang of jealousy as I watch them handle the camera. I bet the New York skyline looks so much more effective in a contrast of black and white tones.

I grimace furiously, annoyed at myself for even entertaining the thought. What am I thinking? I haven't picked up a camera in eleven years. I don't know a thing about photography anymore and I don't want to.

Photography is my past. Taking pictures reminds me of her. That hurts too much for me to even consider picking up a camera again.

I know if I did though, I'd carry on her style. Her photos were beautiful. Are beautiful.

The tourist group moves on and I feel relief wash over me as they fade from view. It is hard to watch people taking pictures.

* * *

I wake up early to the sound of rain cascading down the windows.

"Typical New York," I grumble, wiping my bleary eyes and gazing out of the window.

Work, the last few days, has been dull. Kai has been on a course, so I've been all alone. Normally I use my work as a distraction from real life, but lately it hasn't been working.

As I step through the office doors, Kai greets me as if we haven't seen each other for years. I'm glad to have him back again. He's the only bearable part about this job.

I smile back at him and this time there is nothing forced about it. I'm genuinely happy to see him.

We run through our schedules, comparing and sighing as we work through the task list, before setting a time to grab one of Kai's favourite bagels.

I sit down at my desk and get to work. The morning goes quickly and I feel a lot more productive than normal. Before I know it, I am interrupted by Kai pestering me to go to lunch.

He is half an hour early and I scold him for interrupting my flow, but I don't really mind. His excitement is obvious. I like this Kai. Excited Kai reminds me of childhood, of naivety.

He doesn't speak for the first five minutes, focusing on chewing his bagel. He looks so serious and involved that I don't dare to disturb him.

He often jokes that bagels are his one genuine love (after Tina, of course). I don't think it's a joke.

After he's finished, he becomes his usual self, chatting nonstop as if he'd been away for months, not days.

"So, did you go to the exhibition?" He looks up from over his glass, eyes searching mine for the answer.

I knew this was coming and to be honest, I'm surprised it took him so long to ask. So I tell him everything. Minus Freddie. He seems so genuinely interested, his eyes lighting up every so often when a piece of information catches his imagination.

Lunch with Kai is my favourite time of the workday. So, I'm sad when we have to call it a day and head back to the office.

The afternoon drags on. However, I manage to get into a flow state by mid-afternoon.

"Sydney, I just came to tell you I'm heading home." Kai pokes his head round my door.

"Skiver! It's the middle of the afternoon." I laugh at his bravery. I would never dare to leave this early and I'm the boss's daughter.

"It's three fifty, Syd. I'm surprised you're still here." My face turns pale.

"Three fifty?" I repeat, blinking rapidly.

"Syd? You okay?" Kai looks concerned now as he watches me lean back into the chair and curse under my breath.

"Kai, I feel so bad for asking, but can you drive me to Brooklyn? I have something important to do and I'm about to miss it." I think he senses the desperation in my voice, because he doesn't say a word, simply pulling out his car keys and following me out of the door as I give him the address.

Traffic slows us up and the time ticks by. As we approach the café, my heart begins to pound so hard, I feel it might actually burst through my chest.

"Please say I haven't messed all this up. Please say I haven't missed him." My eyes search the scene in front of me. It's four twenty by the time we eventually come to a stop.

I frantically thank Kai and dive out of his car, waving to him as he drives away, scanning the café. Freddie is nowhere to be seen.

I slump down onto one of their cold iron chairs, willing myself not to cry.

"It's not a big deal. I wasn't even sure about coming here

today. This is probably a blessing." I try to convince myself, failing miserably as I survey the scene in front of me.

Who am I kidding? I feel broken and so guilty. His words were so genuine. He wanted to get to know me and I let him down.

A tear slides down my cheek.

"Sydney?" A voice speaks, calm and clear, from behind me and my heart leaps.

"Freddie."

16

Freddie

I stand in front of the small, cracked mirror in the flat, trying my best to comb through the tangled mess on my head.

"Get a grip, Freddie." I'm nervous to meet her. I don't know why.

I try to remind myself that it is only coffee. We might go our separate ways after this anyway, but somehow I already hope we don't.

As I approach the café, my heart stops. Is she even going to turn up? I haven't heard from her, despite leaving my number, but I try not to let that discourage me.

It's three fifty-five.

I stand outside the café, leaning against the wall, my eyes searching for her continuously.

Four fifteen.

I groan and stand up straight. She isn't coming. I know that at this point I should just leave, but leaving admits defeat and I can't allow myself to give up hope. Not yet. So, I head into the café in search of an extra strong coffee.

Grabbing my drink, I turn once more to face the window. I blink once, then again. She's hurrying out of a car, eyes darting around wildly, searching for me. A look of worry creeps over her face as she turns away, sinking into a chair.

"Sydney?" I ask cautiously.

She spins around to face me and I swear I see her quickly wipe a tear from her cheek as she does.

Was she upset because she thought she had missed me?

"Freddie," she whispers.

"Come on, let's get a table." I grin at her and gesture towards the door as I follow her in, getting her a drink and walking to a table by the window.

"I didn't think you'd come," I admit, looking down at the table and stirring through my coffee.

She looks flustered at this and before long a torrent of apologies erupt from her mouth. "Sorry. I always talk way too much when I'm nervous."

I chuckle and put her at ease. I am so glad she came. We talk like this for what seems like hours. It's natural.

I know neither of us enjoy talking to strangers, but she doesn't feel like a stranger. She never did.

I glance at my phone. It's nearly six. We've been chatting for almost two hours. I wish I could spend more time with her but the sky is fading and I have work in the morning.

I think she notices the time too, because she suddenly goes quiet and gazes out into the darkening sky. Neither of us wants to leave.

"Can I see you again?" Her eyes widen, in anticipation of my response.

"I mean, we don't have to. I know you said in the letter that we might part ways after coffee. So that's okay too, I guess."

She's rambling again now, tugging at her shirt as she looks up at me.

I know it took a lot for her to say that, so I'm going to be brave too.

"How about Monday afternoon? After work? I have somewhere I want to show you."

"Monday is good. Can you meet me from work?"

She really oozes confidence when she lets go and stops overthinking everything. I like that about her. I like that she trusts me enough already to let go, even if it is just a little.

"Sounds good. What's the address?"

She gets up from the table, smoothing her shirt, before looking up and offering me a shy glance.

I follow her out of the door and onto the street as she looks back over her shoulder. "I'll message it to you."

Has she been reading my mind all this time? Does she know that I've been sitting on my phone for days, hoping she'll text me? Of course, she doesn't. But I can't help but smile at the thought of her texting me.

We walk along the darkening Brooklyn streets, continuing our conversation until we reach her street. She tenses as we approach her house, obviously uncomfortable.

"It isn't as good as it looks."

I smile back. She doesn't need to explain anything to me. Not until she's comfortable.

She turns and wanders slowly up the steps to the door. I start to turn to walk away, as her voice pierces the cold air. "I'll text you."

I can't fight the smile that creeps onto my face as I step onto the bridge.

This bridge is the only thing separating Sydney and I now.

This bridge is our gateway.

Ping.

Unknown number.

I must look like an idiot to passers-by as I read her text time and time again, my smile widening.

I feel happy. Not a forced or feigned happy. A true, heart-stopping, joyful, happy. For the first occasion in a long time, I allow myself to dream. Not even the prospect of heading back towards the flat can dampen my spirits now.

My feet pound the pavement and bounce up the steps into the dark hole that is my home. I don't care today though. I collapse onto my mattress and smile at the ceiling, allowing myself to think positively for the first time in years.

Ping.

"Goodnight, Freddie."

17

Freddie

My good mood continues, even as I head into the office I usually hate. Mason's wide grin and bubbly personality doesn't annoy me as much as it usually does. I even allow myself to have a two-minute conversation with him, which I'm sure is a record.

I sit down at my desk and continue to edit and adapt my article ready for review. I'm proud of it. And I can't wait to show Sydney.

The day ticks by slowly. I check the clock every ten minutes.

Despite the constant distraction, Sydney inspires me to keep going and by the time three o'clock rolls round, my article is ready to submit.

I take a wavering breath as I attach the file and write Lucas a quick message underneath. I really hope he likes it.

My job is on the line as I hit the send button. There's nothing more I can do now. He either loves it or he hates it and that's out of my hands.

I gather my things and hurry out of the office. Technically, I shouldn't be leaving yet, but seeing as I have already uploaded my article ahead of time, I am willing to take a chance. Besides, I need to allow myself time to walk over to Sydney's office by three thirty.

A spring takes over my normal, slow steps and my pace increases as soon as I approach her office block.

She's standing outside, talking to an older man, smiling and laughing with him as he gesticulates wildly.

As soon as she spots me, she waves enthusiastically. The man turns around too, confusion crossing his face momentarily as he looks between Sydney and me.

He nods at me politely, a wave of self-consciousness hitting me as I return the gesture.

"See you later, Syd." The man rests his hand on her shoulder before walking back into the office.

"Bye, Kai!" she yells after him, before turning back to me and smiling.

"Ready to go?" I ask, watching as she picks her bag up off the pavement.

She nods, unquestioning.

The conversation flows naturally as we walk, weaving in and out of the crowds, cluttering each stretch of pavement. It feels like I've known her for years.

Her eyes light up as we walk up the steps and onto the highline. "You've never been here before?" I question surprised.

"Nope," she replies sheepishly, looking around in wonder.

"Been here eleven years and I've never really been to Manhattan. I've come here to work or study, that's it." She almost looks ashamed, but there's a guarded nature to her tone, so I decide not to push the issue further.

She looks around in a daze, marvelling at the greenery and plants that surround us.

"Come on. There's a view I think you'll like." We continue to walk and I tell her the history of the highline.

"I've never seen anything so beautiful." Her eyes remain wide the whole time, like she's a child again.

The New York landmark is surrounded by shrubbery, framed by wildflowers. This is my favourite view of the Empire State Building and I'm so glad she loves it.

"I'm sorry the flowers are fading. It's the wrong time of year." I try to explain, but she isn't listening. She seems completely and utterly captivated.

I notice her battling with herself and losing, before she gets her phone out and pokes at the screen.

What is she doing?

She expertly begins fiddling with settings on her phone camera, before pointing it at the view.

So, it's photography that she loves then? I knew it wasn't painting.

She plays with the zoom for a while, before framing the building perfectly with a border of bushes and wildflowers.

That's when I notice it.

The photo she has taken is in black and white.

She stands still for a moment, breathing heavily and staring at the phone in her hand, before turning to me. She looks embarrassed, fearful, even.

"Sorry, let's go." She continues to walk further along the highline, as I break out into a jog to catch up with her.

"Don't apologise. You're a natural." I finally catch up as she turns around to stare at me.

"You really think so?" Her voice is almost inaudible at this point and my heart bleeds for her.

What happened to you, Sydney? What crushed your confidence and left you like this?

I think she regrets asking because she shakes her head. "I'm not a natural." Her eyes flash with that same sadness I recognised outside her house the first time I saw her.

Art triggers the sadness? I try to join the dots, but it is just too complex to understand and I immediately get into a tangle.

We continue to walk, the silence deafening. She still looks sad, but the emotion is slowly being replaced by wonder as we continue to explore.

I see her eyes light up every time she sees something beautiful, but her phone stays firmly in her pocket.

I can tell it is hard for her. There is a hidden story behind the sadness in her eyes. I know there is.

"Hey, Sydney. Look!" I point her toward a group of small birds sitting on a branch next to the fence.

They are beautiful and her eyes light up as she sees them.

She looks over at me, almost looking for confirmation and I nod, watching as she gets her phone out once more. She is a little less hesitant than the first time, as she focuses in on one little guy.

I watch as she concentrates, mesmerised by the way she takes her photos.

She shows me the picture, shyly. It's lovely. It really is.

Why she would hide this kind of talent, I really do not understand. The world should see this. She shouldn't keep it hidden. Yet I can see that she isn't ready to take photos yet let alone share them.

I hope she is ready one day.

"It looks amazing, Sydney!" I swear I see her eyes shine

brighter with the compliment, before putting her phone away again as we continue our walk.

"It really is beautiful here. Why did you bring me to this place? Does it have meaning?" I'm surprised that she asks with so much confidence, but then again, I feel like I know her better after a few days than the people I have known for a lifetime.

I'm not used to speaking about myself. If it was anyone else, I would avoid the question and move on, possibly giving them short shrift on personal privacy. But it isn't someone else. It's Sydney. And I'm starting to trust her.

It's only when I catch her staring at me that I comprehend just how long I have been lost in her eyes.

I look up and place my hand gently against her arm, the fabric of her coat soft to my touch.

"The highline itself is beautiful. I love how peaceful and green it is. A true gem." I begin.

I still haven't removed my hand from her arm, but she hasn't flinched. She doesn't seem to mind.

"But here, underneath this mural, is what is special about this place for me. I come here to think and be at peace." Her eyes glisten as I talk. She understands me. I'm sure of it.

"My special place is the Brooklyn Bridge. I love that it connects Brooklyn and Manhattan. Just sitting on the bridge makes me feel free. Even though I can't really be free." She tails off, staring up at the mural, taking in every inch of its beauty, just like I had done days before.

"I love it," she says eventually, smiling up at me. "It speaks a thousand words."

It's only then I realise how intently I've been staring at her as she studied the mural. I shift my gaze away and back to the wall above.

She is fascinating. I've never met someone seemingly so broken and yet so determined and full of life. I don't even think she knows how to be determined and yet she is.

"Let's stay here a little longer." She pulls me down onto the bench.

The cold is nipping around us, feeling more prominent with every passing second and the evening is drawing in, but I can't say no to her. I don't want to say no to her.

I want to stay here and preserve this moment for as long as is physically possible. So I nod quickly and huddle down into my coat.

My coat itself is tacky and thin and I think she has noticed that because she is looking at me concerned. I really don't want her to know just how dire our financial situation is. Not yet. So, I try to act like the cold isn't bothering me and probably fail miserably.

She loses herself in thought for a while before reaching into her bag and pulling out a bobble hat.

The hat is silver and has sparkles on it. It is the complete opposite of what I would deem manly enough for me to wear and yet she seems determined to get me in it.

I think she knows my answer would be a resounding no if she asked, so she doesn't bother. Instead, she leans over and tries to cram the hat over my head. It fits, but only just and feels tight around my ears.

I can't tell what feels more uncomfortable – wearing the hat or the embarrassment of strangers walking past and seeing me in it.

Sydney seems happy though and finally content that I am warm enough to stay out with her. The concern fades from her face as she studies me, and, to her credit, the hat manages to warm me up.

"I'm sorry if it's too small. Or too sparkly." She looks up at me, trying to stifle a laugh.

I must look ridiculous.

"I haven't bought myself a new hat in ages. I've worn this one for years," she confesses, almost ashamed.

I am not ashamed of her though. The fact that she seems to not throw money after new, pointless items like hats just because they go out of style, makes me happy.

The worry of her being a typical rich girl had faded long ago, but it was still a relief to hear her talk this way.

Maybe she won't judge me like I fear she will? But that isn't a risk I'm willing to take yet.

She's only just given me back the meaning in my life. I can't lose that now.

18

Sydney

We sit on a bench in front of his favourite mural, our chatter breaking through every so often, as we rest in a comfortable silence.

Nothing about being with Freddie feels awkward. It feels right.

He is still wearing my hat and I can't help but think how cute he looks in it, even though it's sparkly and he probably feels embarrassed. I hope it is keeping him warm.

His coat is thin and looks like it needs replacing, but he doesn't complain. I admire that about him.

Cautiously, I reach into my pocket and take out my phone. I adjust the settings and focus to where he is sitting, staring up at the mural.

I capture the first photo.

He is smiling softly. Candid.

"Freddie?" He turns to me and smiles.

Click.

Less candid, but just as meaningful.

My emotions battle within me for a few moments as I look down at the photos in my hand. I haven't taken a picture in so long, but with Freddie I can't seem to stop.

When I'm with him, the world seems so beautiful. New York seems so beautiful and those are words I never thought I'd say.

He doesn't need to say a word his look says it all. He knows and I suddenly feel so exposed.

Throughout my life, my sole purpose has been to keep my secrets hidden. Yet here he is, having spent just days in my life, breaking down those walls stone by stone and unlocking my secrets.

I feel lighter with every minute I spend with him. He understands me.

"We should get going," I whisper, wishing I could take the words back as soon as they leave my mouth.

"Yeah, it's getting late, isn't it?" He looks reluctant, but nods in agreement.

I don't think either of us expected tonight to turn out like this. But I for one am glad it did and I think he is too.

He takes one last fleeting look at his mural and then falls into step by my side.

My life is normally so boring, so routine. This is anything but.

Being out in New York at night is something that would have made the old Sydney feel physically sick. But Freddie makes me feel safe. And being here makes me feel free.

I haven't felt free in so long.

As night rolls in however, I think we both become uneasy. It is a long way back to Brooklyn and I know for a fact that Freddie will want to walk me home, but then I don't want him to walk back alone either.

Freddie goes quiet, processing the options in his head as we continue to walk. It's late and we are now in a predicament, but it was worth it. More than worth it.

* * *

"Morning." Freddie rolls over from his makeshift bed on the floor and looks up at me.

Guilt washes over me once more as I see how uncomfortable he must have been last night. But we didn't have a choice.

My father has a tab here. We use it for late night events and I'm sure he won't care enough to notice one extra night at the end of the month.

We didn't get in till gone eleven last night after sitting and talking for hours. This was the only option.

I don't mind though.

Freddie has a day off and I messaged Kai and told him to let front desk know I was working from home today.

He looks sleepy. His hair is messy and his eyes are tired. I like him like this. He looks natural.

"Breakfast?" He grins at me, flipping through the room service brochure lazily.

We make our choices and before long there is a knock on the door and the familiar scent of the hotel's famous cooked breakfast.

Freddie looks thrilled with his meal as he tucks in. I've never seen anyone eat with so much anticipation and joy.

I turn away before he catches me staring and tuck into my own breakfast, but I can't enjoy it like I usually do. Not when Freddie looks like this is the first and last breakfast he will ever enjoy.

My mind whirs with possibilities and the urge to save him from whatever is causing this pain is all-consuming.

How can I save him if I can't save myself?

* * *

The months fly by and Freddie and I are closer than ever. We both have a lot on with work, but always make time for each other at least twice a week.

Freddie got his proposal accepted by Lucas and it made the front cover of the November issue. As a result, they have given him event after event to cover.

He swears that the Vintage Exhibition is still his favourite coverage though.

I love the article he wrote. It is so meaningful and heartfelt. I kept a copy and hid it in my drawer next to the colour photograph and Little Red Riding Hood.

What about me?

I'm still working in real estate and Kai and I still go out for bagels every lunchtime.

I haven't got back to my mum's storage locker, although I desperately want to. The mystery of what she wanted to tell us is still unsolved and I have a feeling the answer is lost in that locker somewhere.

I'm just too scared to find out, I guess.

For now though, I am content as I can be.

Freddie and I explore New York's street art together at every spare moment. We take joy in the little things, like wandering the streets of the different boroughs. We find happiness in the beauty hidden in the unlikeliest locations.

Oh and I've started writing this journal, just like mum. She was right. It helps to get your emotions and memories down onto paper, so they stay here forever, never fading.

19

Sydney

It is now late March. Freddie and I have known each other for five months. I never thought I would trust anyone enough to call them a friend.

It is normally Freddie who chooses where we go on our days off, but today it is my turn. I spent hours researching the perfect spot and I have finally found it.

Peaceful and secluded. The perfect place to tell him the truth.

Throughout our five months of friendship, both of us have danced around the reasons for our brokenness - fear holding us back. But today I need to be brave.

We walk through the streets in silence. He can sense my apprehension. I'm sure of it.

I go through what I want to tell him in my head repeatedly, even though I know my script will vanish as soon as I speak.

The emotions are too raw, too numbing to be rehearsed and stuck to in that way.

"Central Park?" He looks at me, confused. "I thought we didn't do New York clichés, Syd?"

"We don't," I reply hastily. "You'll see."

For a nice March day, the park isn't as busy as I expected and we weave towards my target with ease.

In the heart of The Ramble, there is a small wooden bench near to a trickling waterfall.

There is no one here.

I sit cross legged on the bench and look around me in wonder. It is so much prettier than I would have ever imagined. The photos don't do it justice.

"This is beautiful, Syd." He gazes around, looking suitably impressed.

I continue to gaze up at the canopy of trees above us as I steady my nerves and get ready to talk.

"I chose this place, because it reminds me of home," I begin, my voice shaky.

He doesn't say a word. He knows this is difficult for me to say. I don't even have to explain what I'm about to tell him. He just knows, placing his hand gently on my knee and giving me a small, reassuring nod.

"New York isn't my home. It never will be. I grew up in the countryside, in England. The perfect childhood, some would say. But it was only perfect because of my mum.

My mum taught me how to photograph, how to see the beauty in things and capture it forever. We would sit together in the darkroom, talking for hours whilst developing our prints.

My mum loved vintage art. Everything she took was in black and white – well, until I found the colour photograph back in October.

She died when I was eleven.

Road accident."

I stop for a moment as I recall the events. Tears are forming at the corners of my eyes and Freddie is staring at me like he's in pain.

He feels my pain.

"When she died, a massive part of me died with her. I packed our photography equipment up into boxes and vowed I would never take another picture ever again.

My love of photography died too that day. But it wasn't just a hobby. It was our foundation.

My mum and I were both bullied throughout our childhoods, although she would never tell me why.

We used our photography to escape into the images, to capture moments that would otherwise fade. It was our safety net.

Not long after that, dad shipped the entire family off to New York.

Hiding our feelings was expected and encouraged and so he threw himself into his work, leaving me to care for me and my sister alone.

I turned into Brianna's mother the second the plane hit the tarmac in JFK. Bri was only five when she passed away and we lost both parents in the space of a month. She couldn't take care of herself, so the duty fell to me.

I associated everything bad in my life with this city. I hated it with every fibre of my being.

Until you.

My life transformed from country living and photography, to part-time carer for Brianna and part time eleven-year-old schoolgirl.

My family wasn't always rich. But my father sold all our assets in the UK, including the teashop my mum loved - the teashop I loved.

He used this money to take a gamble on a real estate firm that needed a partner.

Eleven years later, here we are, living in Brooklyn Heights, the soulless neighbourhood of brown townhouses, where the posh folk live.

That isn't me and it certainly wasn't my father."

At least, I didn't think it was my father. But maybe he was simply good at hiding. I don't know anymore. He has been living a lie for so long I have forgotten what he was really like. Maybe he was just yearning back in England, searching for something more.

"Anyway, I eventually made friends in school. Valentina and Alessia. They made my life slightly more bearable – they still do, but it isn't the same.

My dad doesn't allow us to dream for ourselves. He doesn't even acknowledge Brianna or me ninety percent of the time. She hates him for it, I'm sure. She tries to rebel, go to parties, stay out late, but he never notices. All she wants is for him to notice her. She's only sixteen, Freddie. She shouldn't have to worry about that.

He wants us both in the world of real estate with him. I am an assistant for his firm. Brianna will go through college and then follow. That isn't the life I want for her, though. It isn't the life I want for me either.

I hate it and mum would have hated it too. But I'm trapped. There is no way to escape from this. She is gone and I am broken now. Beyond repair."

Tears stream down my face as I utter the last sentence. I notice a tear slide down Freddie's cheek as his eyes meet mine.

He pulls me against him so I'm practically on his lap. He

holds me tight. It has been years since anyone has cuddled me like this.

My head is resting against his shoulder as I continue to sob. He doesn't seem to care that I'm probably ruining his shirt. He just holds me.

His own breathing is laboured and I can feel his heart racing through the thin fabric of his shirt, as he processes what I've just told him.

"It was my mum's greatest wish for her and me to start a photography business together." I stutter quietly into Freddie's shoulder to break the deafening silence.

"She had a message for her family. I found her account of it in a journal at the storage locker." I pause and steady myself, before daring to utter the words I know will hurt me the most.

"But she died without ever being able to tell us. She died with the conclusion unknown." Fresh waves of tears begin to pour down my cheeks.

"You know, when I was little, my mum used to say I was invincible, that I could do anything in the world. For a while, I believed her. Until I blinked and she slipped away."

He holds me and I swear I feel his heart breaking as I speak those last words. He cares enough about me to allow my story to break his heart.

He eases me away from his shoulder and our eyes lock. "You said something about a storage locker? Maybe the answer is still in there? Maybe her message isn't lost?"

He traces my cheek with his hand, his fingers soft against my skin. "Your mum might have slipped away from you, Syd. But as for her message? I know it's out there somewhere for you to find. We just have to look. And then maybe, with that closure, you can be invincible once more. Just like she wanted

99

you to be."

"I am going to go back. I'm just afraid." He strokes my hair away from my face and catches the tears as they fall.

I have never felt so insecure, but at the same time speaking to him has lifted a weight from my shoulders, shattering it around us on the floor.

I feel lighter.

"I'm afraid that I'll go and I won't find anything and hope really will be lost." The words seem stupid as they fall out of my mouth.

"It's better to have tried and failed, than to never have tried at all Sydney. I can come with you?"

I nod and unsteadily get to my feet, grabbing his hand to pull him up with me. "Let's go."

"What? Now? Are you sure?" I know he is concerned, but I have to know. I need to do this before I change my mind.

"Yes, now."

20

Freddie

I am shaky on my feet as I walk with Sydney through the streets of Manhattan. She still hasn't let go of my hand and is clinging onto me tightly as we walk.

I am trying so desperately hard to stay strong and keep my composure, but it is so difficult. I care about Sydney more than anyone else in the world and seeing her like this makes me want to take that pain away from her, burden it all.

We walk until we reach a door in a small back road. I can't believe Dean would just leave all his wife's things in a locker like this. It isn't even on the right side of the bridge.

She shows her fob to the man on the desk and we head over to the locker. I watch as she punches the number into the grey box.

3074.

Shock hits me as I let my eyes wander around the room. It is nothing more than a prison cell. In fact, I'm sure prison cells are nicer than this.

It is dark, with only a single lightbulb that seems to flicker routinely. My fist clenches involuntarily. I have never met Dean, but I already know that I don't like him.

She sits down on the stone floor, releasing my hand for the first time since we left the bench. It feels empty and cold without her.

"Okay. What are we looking for?" I try to feign confidence, but my voice betrays me and cracks. I know she can tell it's an act.

"Another diary? Letters or notes? I'm not sure, but it will be hidden in amongst the clothes if there is anything." She seems grateful that I'm trying though and manages a small smile.

We get to work, going through every single box with a fine-tooth comb, inspecting everything we find.

A couple of papers are found and discarded, when it transpires that they are only bills or letters with no useful information in them. Each worthless piece of paper found, causes more pain for Sydney, as she loses hope.

Was this a good idea? Maybe I shouldn't have suggested it? This is just going to lead to more distress.

She has finished her pile of boxes. All our hope rests on the remaining few I have yet to search.

Tears begin to shine in her eyes again. Usually I love how her eyes shine. It gives them character and beauty, but not like this.

I put the box I am searching down and scoot over to her. She looks lost.

"We can go. We don't have to do this anymore." Her eyes are empty, void of all feeling, as she stares back at me and processes my words.

"We can't give up now," she replies, hesitantly.

I pull the remaining boxes towards us and search again. Sydney is sitting back now, looking fearful as they diminish.

My fingers brush against something hard. I try to remain calm as I pull the clothes away, not wanting to give Sydney more false hope.

A book rests in my hands. The cover looks old and worn. I show it to Sydney, handing it to her so she can look through it. She doesn't even look though, pushing it straight back to me without a second thought.

"I wouldn't be able to cope if it isn't what we have been looking for." I nod at her and brush the dust from the cover, before opening the book.

It is filled with pages and pages of handwritten memories.

I am sure this is what we have been searching for, but whether it gives her the answers she craves, I don't know.

I hope it does.

"This is it, Syd." I hand it to her to take, but she continues to refuse.

"Will you read bits to me?" She looks terrified. Her hands are shaking and her bottom lip is quivering. I've never seen anyone look this defenceless, not since my mom that night.

I skim through the journal, searching through the dates to find the timeframe. The journal is erratic and only written in occasionally, documenting her journey from childhood into her teenage years.

"Please give Sydney the answers she needs to move on." I take a deep breath and start to read.

January 12, 1986

Mrs Ellington told me I should start a journal. She said that I am a talented writer and I should use it to cope with my emotions.

Today Lydia and her friends made fun of me again. It made me feel sad.

She called me abnormal, a vampire, a freak. She also tried to push me over, but he stopped them.

He is the only friend I have in school and I would be so lonely without him.

The bullying has been getting worse lately, but I don't want to worry mum.

I'm sure it will get better, diary.

I scan through the journal again. There are a lot of entries detailing days out at the beach or taking pictures with her dad.

I tell Sydney in brief accounts, but she is more interested in discovering her mum's secret than finding out about what she had for dinner one Tuesday in June.

July 6, 1989

It is nearly time for the school year to end. I am so happy.

Mum tells me that next year I can leave, help her out at the shop part-time and take photos.

I will miss him, though. He is the only person who has been keeping me going these last few years.

He understands me and my situation. We have become the best of friends.

He helps me stand up to my bullies when they call me wobbly eyes or mock me for not being able to go outside at break times.

He always stays inside with me. We go to the library.

I know I shouldn't complain. I don't have it half as bad as the other case studies I read about, but it still makes me unhappy.

I don't want to be different, not like this.

My heart is aching for Eden in this moment. Whatever she

is going through is affecting her more than words can say. Her pain radiates through the page.

July 20, 1990

I've done it! I finally get to leave school!

I can't wait to start working in the teashop. She says that one day it could be mine. And that is so exciting!

But I want to be a photographer full time. That is my dream.

The hardest part about today was saying goodbye to him.

He is moving away, not just to a different county, but a different country, halfway around the world from me.

He is off, following his dreams and I know I should be happy for him. But it was a bittersweet moment.

He has been my guiding light for years.

What will I do without him?

He kissed me goodbye, just before he left for the airport and I cried a lot.

He told me not to worry, that he would be back. College would only last a few years and then he would be back – for good.

He promised he would come back for me. I hope he does diary, I really do.

I can't help but note how much this friendship sounds like us. I would fall apart if Sydney ever left me. I think I know how Eden felt in that moment.

June 10, 1992

He didn't come back to me, diary. That day at the airport, he promised.

This date has been marked in my calendar ever since that moment, but he hasn't arrived.

I had to go to the doctor today, for a usual check-up.

I hate the doctors.

The conversation is always along the lines of how lucky I am to just have incomplete achromatopsia.

"If you had complete achromatopsia, you wouldn't be able to function without help. You are lucky, Eden."

I hate Doctor Murray.

Today, I was particularly irritable. He hadn't come back to me and I was stuck in a doctor's office.

Damned, achromatopsia.

If I didn't have it. Who knows? Maybe he would be here now? Maybe he wouldn't have left me? Maybe he would have loved me like I love him?

But he doesn't. He isn't here.

I'm an abnormality.

I am never telling anyone I meet in my future about my condition.

I am determined to keep it hidden. I don't want to suffer anymore. It isn't fair.

I want to be Eden. Not Eden with the eye problem.

Just, Eden.

My heart stops and I look up from the page and shift my gaze to Sydney.

Incomplete achromatopsia? What even is that?

Her mouth is wide open, her face flushed with complete and utter shock. She can't cry. She can't even utter a word. She just sits still.

"There are just two more entries, Syd. From years later."

October 1, 1997

He came back to me.

It was amazing to see him after all this time.

I barely recognised him as he walked through the door of the teashop.

America has changed him. But he is still the same boy I loved years before.

He says he's only going to be in town a few days. He just wanted to come back and see me before he left again.

He doesn't know when he'll be back, if at all, but I'm happy for him.

He has a great job and is making something of himself.

I'm only thankful to have known him.

To have spent years in his company.

This friend must have been something special. I am pleased Eden got her closure in amongst all of these tragic entries.

At least she got this one small victory.

December 19, 1997

This is going to be my last journal entry.

Writing in it doesn't seem the same now he's gone. This book follows our journey, but he isn't coming back.

So, this chapter is closed. I have Dean now.

I'm expecting my first baby.

He's excited, but I'm afraid. I'm excited to meet my baby, don't get me wrong, but right now, I just get the feeling that nothing will ever be the same again.

As soon as the words escape my mouth, I regret saying them. This just throws up more question marks for Sydney and we've exhausted every box in this locker. There are no more answers lurking around in these depths.

I smile and try to reassure her. "Your first child is a massive deal, Syd. I'm sure she was just apprehensive."

She looks relieved at this response and I'm glad. The last thing she needs is more unanswered questions.

21

Sydney

Incomplete achromatopsia.

So, my mum had an eye condition?

I can't believe she was too afraid to tell us. Her own family.

I can sense Freddie staring at me, concerned, but for the moment I just want to be alone.

I pull out my phone and type into Google.

'Incomplete achromatopsia is where colour vision is impaired, but not totally absent.'

'Symptoms are milder, but not non-existent. They are easier to control than complete achromatopsia.'

Seeing the words right there, in black and white, made it feel so real. My mum was suffering.

Wait.

Black and white?

My mum took me out to photograph at dusk, never before. She only took her photos in black and white.

Now I know why.

It was so she could see the true effects of their beauty.

She would always tell me I brought the colour into her life. I thought it was just a figure of speech.

Her colourless photography was her way of expressing herself. It was her way of trying to show the world what she was going through, without fear of being judged like she had previously been.

How could someone develop the strength and courage to keep something like that hidden for all that time?

I know I couldn't do it.

How did I never guess? Or see that something was wrong?

"Sydney?"

I hadn't even noticed Freddie moving closer to me, wrapping his arms around me.

I hadn't noticed the tears start to fall.

I hadn't even noticed my legs turn cold against the bare concrete of the locker floor.

I lean my head back into Freddie's shoulder.

"I don't want to go home tonight," I whisper into the cold air. "I can't face my dad, or Brianna. Not now."

"You don't have to go anywhere you don't want to, Sydney." His tone is calm and reassuring, but I know inside he is falling apart.

"You know, I think your mum would be so proud of who you turned out to be." He turns my head gently and gets me to look up at him as he continues.

"Just from reading her journal, I see so much of her in you. She was an incredibly special woman. So are you."

No one has ever been this nice to me before. It is overwhelming.

"Hey, Syd. Don't cry." His face contorts as he watches a single tear rocket down my cheek, adding to the red blotches

110